STAR WARS

JEDI QUEST

THE FINAL SHOWDOWN

JEDI QUEST

CHOSEN BY FATE.
DESTINED FOR CONFLICT.

JEDI QUEST

BY JUDE WATSON

THE FINAL SHOWDOWN

SCHOLASTIC INC.

New York   Toronto   London   Auckland   Sydney
Mexico City   New Delhi   Hong Kong   Buenos Aires

www.starwars.com
www.scholastic.com

ISBN 0-439-33926-X

12 11 10 9 8 7 6 5 4 3 2   5 6 7 8 9/0

Printed in the U.S.A.
First printing, November 2004

JEDI QUEST

THE FINAL SHOWDOWN

CHAPTER ONE

"Power cell?"

"Check."

"Reserve?"

"Check."

"Blade crystals?"

A glowing shaft buzzed to life.

"All check," Tru Veld said. He turned his lightsaber around, looking at the flame-colored ray. It gave his silvery skin a rosy tint.

"I adjusted the flux aperture for you and rebalanced the handle," Anakin Skywalker told him.

"Feels great." Tru deactivated the lightsaber and tucked it into his belt. "Thanks. I may have built this lightsaber, but you sure keep it humming." Tru looked down at his utility belt. "Liquid cable — check. Comlink —

check. Aquata breather — check. And . . ." Tru reached into a small slit in his belt and withdrew a small bag. He swung it in the air. "Mmmm . . . some Terratta to eat on the ride."

"Check." Anakin caught the snack Tru tossed to him and popped it in his mouth. "Obviously, you've thought of everything."

The two teenage Padawans eased down on the floor and passed the food back and forth. They had checked each piece of equipment five times now. They knew everything was functional, but they kept on checking. Routine kept their nerves steady.

Many Jedi now had to be ready to leave at a moment's notice. Throughout the Temple, Jedi Knights were finishing up last-minute assignments and gathering their gear for new ones. Apprentices said good-bye to friends and fellow learners. Information was uploaded onto datascreens. Starfighters and cruisers were standing by, ready and fueled.

Just days before, there had been an attack on the Senate. Twenty-one Senators had been killed, along with twenty-four aides and guards. The numbers would have been higher if the Jedi had not been alerted. Even Supreme Chancellor Palpatine had been in danger. His life had been saved by Ferus Olin, Tru and Anakin's fellow apprentice.

The attacks had been carried out by Granta Omega and Jenna Zan Arbor, notorious galactic criminals. Yet the Jedi Council believed that a Sith was the real power behind the terrible plan and the Senate feared that this first attack was only the beginning of a much wider plot. They did not want to simply wait for the next attack. The idea was to spread a wide net, check out old sources of information, and develop new ones to lure in and trap the criminals.

Chancellor Palpatine urged restraint. Galactic politics were volatile, and he needed a period of calm to steady the mood of the Senate, which had grown ugly since the attack. He cautioned the Jedi to be discreet.

Whatever the next step, Anakin felt confident that he would be involved. His Master, Obi-Wan Kenobi, had been the first Jedi to warn the Council about Granta Omega's plans. His Master knew the evil villain better than anyone, and he would be on the team sent to bring Omega to justice. Tru was hoping that he and his Master, Ry-Gaul, would be sent as well.

Suddenly a head peeked around the corner of Anakin's quarters. "Terratta strips? And nobody invited me?" Darra Thel-Tanis held out a hand and the bag sailed into it, with the help of the Force.

"Show off," Tru said, grinning.

Darra slid down onto the floor next to her friends.

She chewed on the candy with vigorous appreciation. Darra did everything with gusto. She had always been a vivid presence among the apprentices, with the bright bits of fabric she weaved through her auburn Padawan braid and her wisecracking manner.

But Anakin could feel a new maturity in her, a hardened sense of purpose. Ever since she'd been wounded on Haariden, she seemed to carry a sense of gravity along with her humor. She'd told Anakin that the incident had brought death so close that she'd made friends with it. The remark had been a joke, but a joke that vibrated with a seriousness Anakin had trouble accepting. He sometimes wanted the old Darra back, whose jokes were simply jokes, not keys to her own sorrows.

"Something's up," Darra said. "Your Masters are both in the Council room."

This was news to Anakin and Tru. They exchanged a glance.

"Soara is in there, too," Darra continued, speaking of her own Master. "I have a feeling we'll be leaving the Temple before the day is out." She stretched out her legs. "I'm ready."

"Was Siri Tachi there?" Tru asked.

"I saw her go in with Ferus," Darra said, nodding.

"With Ferus?" Anakin asked. A jolt of jealousy made him straighten. "Why is Ferus there when we're not?"

Darra shrugged. "They asked for him. Rumors are going around — something about the apprentices. I don't know what."

"But why is Ferus there?" Anakin asked again.

Darra shot him a curious look. "Do I look like a Council member? Moons and stars, I hope I'm not that grim. You're just going to have to wait and find out."

"I don't think it will be long," Tru said, trying to reassure Anakin. Tru was Anakin's best friend, and he knew that Anakin and Ferus had clashed in the past. Although they got along better now, there was still a rivalry between them.

Just then, all three of their comlinks buzzed at the same time.

Darra consulted her message. "Well, whatever it is, we're about to find out."

Anakin was used to standing in the Council room by now. He wasn't nervous, the way he'd been as a ten-year-old refugee from Tatooine. He was almost nineteen now, close to being a Jedi Knight. Yet still, this time something was different. He felt a heavy presence in the room. The Council members sat in their various chairs, waiting for the three Padawans to step forward next to their Masters. Usually Anakin could count on a nod or a smile from a Council member or two, but today everyone looked, as Darra had said, grim. He felt the Force in the room, humming underneath and through them. He imagined that this concentration of energy was similar to what a war council might feel like.

Ferus stood to one side, next to Siri. He did not look at Anakin, or at the other Padawans. Something trickled down Anakin's neck, a foreboding he didn't want to name. Suddenly he had a feeling that he wasn't going to like what he was about to hear.

"And now, to begin," Mace Windu said, once the Padawans had taken their places. "First, the Council wishes to apologize to Master Kenobi, who has warned us many times of the danger of Granta Omega. We did not take the warnings as seriously as they were given. You were right, Obi-Wan. Omega should have been our first priority. He is now."

Obi-Wan nodded.

"You will be the first Jedi coalition to go after him," Mace said, looking at each of the Masters and Padawans in turn. "You may contact the Temple at any time to ask for any degree of help or any number of Jedi to join you. We leave these decisions to you. The Council feels that there is Sith involvement, but to what degree we do not know. Therefore we urge each of you to weigh every move you make with care."

Mace steepled his fingers together. "We have located Granta Omega and Jenna Zan Arbor."

Anakin saw his Master give a start.

"They are on Korriban."

Anakin felt the dread in the room. He knew of Korriban only through legends. Thousands of years before, it had been the seat of Sith power. The tombs of the ancient Sith Lords were there, and it was still a source of the dark side of the Force. It was a place no Jedi wanted to go.

"Of course," Obi-Wan said. "He has strived to be noticed by the Sith, and at last he has succeeded. Now he goes for his reward."

"Whatever that may be," Mace agreed. "Certainly protection is part of it." Mace's intense gaze moved from Tru to Darra until it came to rest on Anakin. "And now we come to a piece of news for the Padawans. Because of our concern for the state of the galaxy and evidence that the dark side of the Force is gathering, the Council has made a decision to speed up the process of apprentices becoming Jedi Knights."

Anakin found it difficult to keep his face neutral as excitement surged through him. He knew what was coming. He was going to be allowed to undertake the trials!

He was ready. He was more than ready.

"This is a major decision, and so we have decided to proceed cautiously, with one test case," Mace went on.

Anakin's heart swelled. Of course it would be him. He was the Chosen One, the one with the greatest skills, the greatest Force connection.

"After much discussion, and consultation with all Jedi Masters, the Council has chosen Ferus Olin as the first Padawan to undergo the trials. After this mission, he will begin the trials."

For a moment, Anakin heard nothing, just a blank where his name should have been. The words *Ferus Olin* seemed to have no meaning, like they were part of a language he hadn't learned. That was how unreal it felt.

He wanted to move, wanted to cry out. This couldn't be true! It couldn't be happening!

He glanced at his Master. Obi-Wan was looking at Yoda.

"We want to make it clear that our decision, while unanimous, doesn't reflect on any Padawan's fitness to be a Jedi Knight. We believe in each of you. Yet we had to choose someone, and this is a way to begin. You will each be ready in your own time."

My time is now! Anakin wanted to shout. Disbelief and anger coursed through him.

Mace rose. "The ships are ready for your journey to Korriban. May the Force be with you."

Anakin did not know how he was going to get out of the room without exploding. His emotions were too wild to control. It was only by hanging on to the habit of a life of discipline that he was able to turn and follow his Master out of the room. Ahead of him strode Ferus, the thick gold stripe in his hair catching the light of the glow rods overhead. First out of the Council room. First on the list.

Ferus.

CHAPTER TWO

"Don't say anything," Obi-Wan said in a low tone. "Follow me."

Anakin's face was hot. He followed his Master through the hallway and onto the turbolift. He watched the levels count off as he slowed his breaths, fighting for control.

Obi-Wan led the way out of the turbolift and into the Room of the Thousand Fountains. Anakin knew his Master had chosen this site deliberately. The soft splash of the fountains were a calming aid to all Jedi. The room smelled of green growth, and the refracted light of the water gave the air a soft radiance.

None of this worked to calm him. He wanted to fight against it.

"How did it happen?" Anakin asked, as soon as he

was sure they were alone. "How *could* it happen? I don't understand!"

"Anakin, of course you're disappointed," Obi-Wan said. "It is natural to want to be first."

"I *am* first!" Anakin exploded. "I was always first in my class. First in lightsaber training. First in the Force."

Obi-Wan frowned. "There is no such thing. We don't rank students at the Temple."

"That is what is *said*," Anakin answered. "But it's not the reality, and you know it."

Obi-Wan took a breath. "How good you are is not the point."

"What makes Ferus better?"

"That is not the point either. The fact is he is *ready!*" Obi-Wan's voice was raised, and that didn't happen very often. Anakin could see that he was pushing his Master to the limit.

But he couldn't stop. Not on something that was this important to him. "I'm ready!" he insisted. "I'm just as ready as he is."

"That is something you cannot know," Obi-Wan said, shaking his head. "It is not for the Padawan to know. It is for the Master and the Council."

Obi-Wan's words stopped Anakin in his tracks. A sudden knowledge seared his brain.

"You *agreed* with them," he said. "You voted for Ferus!"

"It was not a vote . . ." Obi-Wan began.

"You agreed —"

"It was a discussion," Obi-Wan interrupted. "To which all Masters were invited."

"You're not answering me."

Obi-Wan paused. "Yes. I agreed with the Council's choice."

Anakin felt as though he had received a sharp prod from an electrojabber.

"Anakin." Obi-Wan made a move to put his hands on Anakin's shoulders, but did not actually touch him, knowing somehow that Anakin would push him off. "This is not about your skills, your commitment, or your abilities. This is about whether you are *ready*. There is a difference."

"You don't think I'm ready." Anakin could hear how wooden his voice sounded.

"I think Ferus is. That does not mean I think he will make a better Jedi. It only means that I think he is ready now."

Ferus had manipulated them. Ferus had somehow made this happen. He had voiced his doubts about Anakin aloud, sometimes in front of his Master, and somehow he had corrupted their opinions of him.

Anakin's fury grew until it was something wild, something he did not know if he could contain. He looked at his Master, and suddenly Obi-Wan was a stranger to him.

"I can feel your anger," Obi-Wan said. "Take care."

He did not want to take care. He wanted to punch something.

"Your focus on who gets to be Master first is only reinforcing the rightness of the Council's decision," Obi-Wan went on. "You're treating this like a contest. You are not emotionally ready to be a Jedi. Decisions like this must be accepted."

"You do not need to quote Jedi teachings," Anakin said through his teeth. "I know them well. Better even than Ferus, though that doesn't seem to make a difference."

Obi-Wan's face was tight. "You need a little time to compose yourself. We can discuss this further if you like. I'll leave you now."

Obi-Wan turned away. His shoulders were tense. He took a few steps, then relented. He turned back.

"I believe in you, Anakin," he said.

Anakin had turned, too, and now kept his back to his Master. He could not answer him. He could only think of Ferus. After a moment, he heard Obi-Wan leave the room.

Ferus had plotted. Ferus had beaten him. Ferus had won.

And now he had to work with him on this mission. He had to help Ferus achieve what he, Anakin, deserved. He imagined Ferus's smug face as he accepted the praise of the Council. As he took his place as a Jedi Knight. He imagined Ferus as a Knight and himself still a Padawan.

It can't happen that way.

Anakin took his anger and focused it. For a moment, the water from the many fountains around him hung suspended in the air. He used the Force to keep the water frozen in midair, just to prove he could do it. The silence filled his ears. Then he let it fall, all the fountains gushing, trickling, racing once again. The noise seemed enormous now, a torrent. As though he could hear every drop of water hit every pebble.

Anakin felt a surge of power. This was only a part of what he was capable of. Soon they would all know it. He would show them that they had made a serious mistake. He should be the first apprentice to move up to Jedi Knight. He knew it. And soon everyone else would know it, too.

He would make them know it.

CHAPTER THREE

The Jedi assembled in the vast hangar in front of the two Republic cruisers they would take to Korriban. They split up the teams, with Siri and Obi-Wan in one cruiser with their Padawans, Soara and Ry-Gaul and their Padawans in the other. That way, the two best pilots in the group — Anakin and Ry-Gaul — would be in different ships.

Obi-Wan wished it could be otherwise. He didn't think it wise to put Anakin and Ferus together in a small cruiser until Anakin had cooled down. He had no choice, however; every decision they made from now on could be a crucial one. They had to think every step through. It was entirely possible that they would be attacked on the journey. They couldn't take anything for granted anymore.

While Anakin and Ry-Gaul did a flight check on their vehicles, Obi-Wan studied his fellow Jedi. It had been six years since they had all been together on a mission. The past years had been long and hard, and they all looked more focused, more intent, than they had all those years before when they went to patrol the Galactic Games.

Obi-Wan knew that Tru and Ry-Gaul had been on a series of highly dangerous missions and that Soara and Darra were recently caught in the middle of a fierce interplanetary war. He saw the changes in all the Padawans, how their faces reflected the seriousness of their purpose and the things they had seen. He saw in them the same recognition that he had once faced, as he had come to the end of his years of apprenticeship. You started out as a Padawan thinking you would lead a life of service and adventure, and you pictured your successes to come, not your failures. Successes could be daydreamed about in a vague way, but failures were more particular. They couldn't be envisioned. With the years you accumulated not only satisfactions but also disappointments and heartbreaking losses. Imprinted in your memory were things you wished you had not seen. The Jedi path was more complicated than you'd ever dreamed as you polished your lightsaber hilt and yearned to be chosen.

Siri was leaner, if that was possible. Her edge was sharper. Obi-Wan saw less of her humor and more of her frustration.

Ry-Gaul's bleached gray eyes seemed even paler, as if his experiences had leached out the color. Now they were almost white. He spoke even less now. When Obi-Wan had asked him about it, Ry-Gaul had fixed his moon-colored eyes on him and said, "There is less to say."

Soara Antana, oddly, had grown softer, almost tender, with Darra. Darra herself seemed the same, though the exuberance that danced in her unusual, rust-colored eyes would sometimes shift to a shadowy sadness.

And what of himself? What did his fellow Jedi think of him? He caught sight of his bearded face in the reflection of the windscreen. He was not old. He was younger than Qui-Gon had been when he took him on as a Padawan. Yet he felt old. In his bones, he felt a strange weariness. It was the concentration of all the effort he placed in vigilance. In watching. Waiting for something he could not name.

They all felt it. A gathering of the dark side of the Force. They held out their hands, pushing against the darkness, the chaos. They were tired, and they had so much farther to go.

And now, Anakin. He had to count on Anakin's maturity, the integrity of his core. Anakin would forgive him for supporting Ferus. It had been difficult for Obi-Wan himself to admit that Ferus was the best candidate. Naturally he'd wanted Anakin to be chosen, but something had held him back. He couldn't have done it if he hadn't felt the times were too perilous for the Jedi to make a mistake.

In time, Anakin would find acceptance. Obi-Wan was confident this was so, because he knew Anakin so well. He knew that Anakin was struggling now, and he knew that he could not help him. He knew Anakin's better side would win.

To Obi-Wan's surprise, Yoda himself suddenly appeared, gliding in his repulsorlift chair from the turbolift. Obi-Wan walked forward quickly to greet him on the landing platform.

"Master Yoda, is something wrong?"

Yoda did not answer him. Instead, Obi-Wan watched as Yoda's gray-blue eyes moved from one Jedi to another in turn, lingering on the faces of the Padawans.

"Felt I did that look upon you all before you left I must," Yoda said. "And tell you . . ."

"Yes, Master?"

Another pause. Then Yoda leaned on his gimer stick and frowned. "Like Ry-Gaul, I have become. Nothing to say, I have." Now he gazed with great affection at Obi-Wan. "What I would say, know you do already."

And Obi-Wan did. A great dread lay inside Yoda. He needed to look at them in case they did not all come back. He needed to stand here and watch them go so they would know how deeply he felt for them. He wanted to see them off, see the last glint of sun on a wing as they flew.

Obi-Wan nodded.

"Checks completed," Anakin called, and Ry-Gaul gave a thumbs-up.

The Jedi turned to board.

"May the Force be with you," Yoda said. He lifted one three-fingered hand in good-bye.

CHAPTER FOUR

Obi-Wan sat in front of the nav computer. There was nothing to do; they had been in hyperspace for days now, and they were approaching Korriban within the Horuset system. He knew their position exactly, and how far they needed to go. Still he continued to check coordinates and try to foresee potential problems. It was what he'd always done, even as an apprentice. He found comfort in the routine of it.

The journey had passed without incident. Ferus had kept a delicate distance between himself and Anakin, delicate because he gave distance without seeming to. Obi-Wan appreciated this effort. Ferus had given Anakin space, and that was not easy on such a small cruiser.

Siri came up behind him. "If you check that space chart once more, you're going to burn out the screen."

Obi-Wan spun around in his chair. "It never hurts to triple check."

"It hurts *me*," Siri said. Her keen blue eyes glinted at him. "All that precision gives me the shivers."

Obi-Wan grinned, then pressed the button for holo-mode. The star chart hovered in the air. "There it is," he said, indicating Korriban. "So isolated that it makes up its own system. Marooned in space, as though the other planets have chosen to hide from it."

Siri sat astride a chair, planting her hands on her knees. "Don't be so poetic. It's just a planet."

"More than a planet," Obi-Wan said, gazing at the chart. "A source of evil that still calls evil to come meet it."

"I don't believe that," Siri said. "It's just a place where some old Sith bones lie."

"The Valley of the Dark Lords," Obi-Wan said. They had heard of the valley from their earliest days as students at the Temple, had used tales of the valley to scare each other as younglings. "The dark side of the Force still lives in that valley. Korriban has never recovered from the Sith occupation. That was thousands of years ago, and yet the planet has never formed a government or attracted settlers. It's not part of the galactic alliance. It has never joined the Senate."

Siri rose to study the holo-chart more closely. "Even freighters won't stop there," she murmured. "And freighters stop everywhere." As she moved to the opposite side of the chart, briefly, the image of Korriban was reflected on her face. She shuddered and moved away.

Siri sat back down opposite Obi-Wan. "The Commerce Guild has opened an office there," she observed.

"They're offering incentives to get corporations to open branches in the Dreshdae spaceport," Obi-Wan said. "I've been studying the files. Of course it is a world with no taxes, and that's a Commerce Guild issue, but it's still strange."

"They are just trying to gain influence on major corporations," Siri said. "Keep them in their backyard so they can control them. It's the same old dance."

"But Korriban?" Obi-Wan mused. "There has to be a reason . . . the Sith might be behind it, even if the Commerce Guild doesn't know it."

Siri waved a hand. "Then they'll get what they deserve."

While they were talking, the Padawans slowly drifted closer to join the conversation.

"So who is living on Korriban?" Ferus now asked.

"Three types of beings," Siri replied, checking them off on her fingers. "One, those who are forced to live there because of work. Two, those who have been stranded there. Three, those who choose to be there."

"Those are the dangerous ones, no doubt," Obi-Wan said.

"How are we going to find Omega?" Anakin asked. "Dreshdae isn't large, but he and Zan Arbor will be in hiding. And Korriban is huge. They could be hiding out anywhere."

"I don't think he's come to Korriban to hide," Obi-Wan said. "He's come for a reason. My guess is that he's been invited. He's succeeded in his goal — he's attracted the notice of the Sith. He's going there for his reward."

"More wealth?" Siri asked. "He certainly doesn't need it."

"Maybe help with his next plan," Ferus said. "He could need weapons, ships, droids . . . we don't know."

Obi-Wan nodded. "True."

The instrument panel showed they were about to come out of hyperspace. It was time to enter the coordinates for landing at Dreshdae.

Obi-Wan drifted to the front of the cockpit and the others followed. They stood, looking out into dark space. There were few stars out here, and no planets. Korriban loomed in their vision, a large planet with blood-red clouds obscuring its surface.

"I've heard it called the cradle of darkness," Obi-Wan said. He realized that he had lowered his voice.

He felt it now, the dark side of the Force emanating from the planet's surface. Looking at the faces of the Jedi, he knew they felt it as well. It had a sick sweetness to it, something that seemed to pour through his veins, attracting and repelling him at once. It was the most complicated surge of the dark side he had ever felt.

He struggled to meet it, struggled to clear his mind.

Warily, Obi-Wan moved forward and entered the coordinates into the nav computer. His fingers hesitated even as they entered the data. It was as though making the commitment to land was sealing their fate.

He stood and joined the other Jedi at the cockpit windscreen. They couldn't turn away. The ship flew into the atmosphere, straight through the blood-red clouds, and dread entered their hearts as the surface of the planet grew closer.

CHAPTER FIVE

He would have to wear a mask. A mask of friendship. Anakin had decided this before he'd left the Temple. Ferus could never know his true feelings. He would defeat him without Ferus ever knowing they were in competition.

That had been his plan, but it was hard to follow through when faced with Ferus himself. Anakin could feel his resentment leaking out like a gas. It was only a question of time before he exploded.

No. I will prove I am a better Jedi. I will not explode in anger.

They flew over the planet, over mountain ranges and desert and deep canyons.

"Where is the Valley of the Dark Lords?" Ferus asked.

"Invisible from the air," Obi-Wan told him. "The valley is narrow, a slit hidden in the mountains some distance from Dreshdae. Plus it is constantly under heavy cloud cover."

"There's the spaceport," Siri said, as it loomed closer.

Dreshdae had been built on a plateau in the middle of the largest mountain range on the planet. From the air, the Jedi could see a huddle of buildings cramped together with no effort at orderly design.

The landing platform was deserted except for a small number of cruisers behind an energy fence. There was no one to check them in and no one to care. The landing area itself had been recently refurbished, but it had been a hasty job and already the platform was pitted and scarred.

Soara, Darra, Ry-Gaul, and Tru came over to Anakin's ship once they had landed. The Masters huddled in the cockpit, going over some last-minute details. The Padawans stood on the ramp, looking out over the spaceport and preparing their equipment. Dreshdae looked as grim at ground level as it had from the air.

"Not exactly Belazura," Darra said as she stuffed her thermal cape into her survival pack.

"I've seen worse," Ferus said. "I hope."

Ferus might have meant the remark as a joke, but

Anakin took it as a challenge. Ferus was showing off again.

"We all have," Anakin pointed out.

"I don't think so," Tru said. "I'd say we've finally made it to the worst the galaxy has to offer." He said this cheerfully as he wound one flexible arm around his back to fasten the strap on his survival pack. As a Tee-van, Tru could bend his limbs backward and twist them in surprising angles. It was one of the things that made him such an excellent fighter.

"I don't think you'll be finding any Terratta strips here," Darra teased Tru. "I have a feeling we'll be living on food capsules. I wouldn't trust the food on this planet."

"I never get the good planets," Tru whined, making a comical face.

They were joking now, wanting to displace the odd tension they all felt.

"We've come a long way from the Galactic Games, that's for certain," Ferus said. "Remember how nervous we were on our early missions?"

"Sure," Tru said. "I still am." He looked out at Dreshdae, and the humor drained from his face. "Especially here."

"What about you, Ferus?" Anakin asked as he bent over to tighten a strap that didn't need tightening. "Nervous? Or is that not allowed for a Jedi Knight?"

"I'm not a Jedi Knight yet," Ferus answered.

"But you're closer than any of us," Anakin said, straightening. "Does that make you more nervous or less? I mean, let's face it, the Jedi Council's eyes are on you."

Ferus frowned as he picked up the taunt buried in Anakin's easy tone. "I'm not thinking about that. I'm thinking about the mission."

"We're all thinking about the mission, Anakin," Darra said.

"Of course, we all want to capture Omega," Tru added. His eyes told Anakin to back off.

"But Ferus wants to be the one to do it, I'll bet," Anakin said. "Once you start impressing the Jedi Council, you have to keep on doing it."

"It doesn't matter who does it," Ferus said. "It matters that it's done."

"Spoken like a true Jedi Knight," Anakin said.

Ferus's neck flushed red. "Just what are you trying to say?"

"Anakin —" Darra murmured warningly.

Anakin took a step closer to Ferus. He couldn't help himself. Despite his best intentions, the words spilled out in a torrent. "That you'll do whatever you can to succeed on this mission, but not because you want to catch Omega. You want to be a Knight."

"Anakin!" Tru exclaimed.

But Ferus and Anakin were past listening to their fellow Padawans. They were careful to pitch their voices low, however, to avoid attracting the attention of their Masters.

Ferus's dark eyes flashed with anger. "That's a serious charge, and an untrue one."

"I've got news for you," Anakin said. "You won't be the one to find Omega. I will. I'd bet on it." The remark seemed to burst out of him without his directing it.

Darra sucked in a breath through her teeth. Tru shook his head.

Ferus turned away. "I'm not going to bet on a mission."

"Because you have too much riding on it? If you lose, you might lose the Council's favor," Anakin said. "No wonder you won't take me up on it."

Anakin had gotten to Ferus at last. He could see it. Suddenly Ferus spun around and came within centimeters of Anakin.

"Okay, sure, I'll take the bet," he said. "Whatever you say, Anakin. I wouldn't want to stand in the way of you and your ego."

"Ego? You're the one who spends all his time showing off!"

But if Anakin was heat, Ferus was ice. He buckled

his utility belt. "Someone has to teach you that you are not as powerful as you think you are."

Anakin saw the Masters looking over. He bent over and pretended to tighten the same tight strap so that Obi-Wan could not read his face. He had to control himself. He had gone farther than he'd meant to, but he didn't care. Now it was out in the open.

They followed their Masters out onto the main thoroughfare of Dreshdae, a narrow unpaved street. A light gray rain was falling, and it had an acid taste. Anakin felt foreboding settle on his shoulders.

Dreshdae was a hodgepodge, a drab spaceport that had grown and shrank without regard for utility or beauty. Until recently it had been a collection of temporary buildings made of plastoid blocks or cheaper metals that rusted with age. The Jedi could see these buildings in various states of disrepair. Sprung up around them was a collection of newer buildings, most of them clustered near the Commerce Guild's Dreshdae Headquarters. The Guild had spared no expense, building a multistoried edifice with durasteel facing in a multicolored iridescence that was supposed to sparkle in sunlight but instead looked cheerless in the drip of rain.

Although Dreshdae tried to present itself as a typical

new, brash city struggling to grow, the strain showed. There was no disguising what the spaceport had been and would slide back into again — a dark, dangerous, lawless place. Undercurrents of its evil past bubbled up through the cracks in the stone facings and the hastily erected walkways. Beings hurried through the streets as if anxious to find shelter. No one lingered in the cafés. Anakin didn't hear one snatch of conversation, or one burst of laughter.

"Our contact is a businessman named Teluron Thacker," Obi-Wan said. "He's done favors for the Jedi in the past, and he agreed to help us if he could. The meeting place isn't far."

Anakin felt a touch on his shoulder and turned. No one was behind him. Perhaps it had been a leaf brushing his shoulder — but he knew, of course, that there were no trees on Korriban.

Another touch — Anakin whipped around. He looked at Ferus, wondering if he was trying to play a trick on him, but Ferus was several meters back, talking to Soara.

He began to pick up a whisper. Then another. He couldn't make out the words, only the intent. Someone was baiting him, cajoling him, laughing at him . . . or was it his imagination? Was it just the wind whispering through the stones?

They crossed the street and he thought he saw a flash of something — blood coursing down a stone wall. When he blinked, it was gone.

"Master . . . "

"It is the dark side of the Force, Anakin," Obi-Wan said. "I'm picking it up, too. Ignore it."

But Anakin couldn't ignore it. There was something insistent about the voices. Something that urged him to answer. Although the feeling made him anxious, he also wanted to face it. He wanted to get to the root of this dark power . . . to match himself against it . . . to prove, once and for all, that he was as strong as it was.

CHAPTER SIX

Obi-Wan stopped outside the small café. It fit the coordinates he was given, but still he hesitated. Was it even open? The café was small, dingy, and in serious disrepair. Half of the roof was caving in. It was a wonder anyone would go inside at all.

"What is it, Master?" Anakin asked.

"Teluron Thacker is a prosperous businessman," Obi-Wan said. "Why would he frequent this kind of place?"

"You think it's a trap?"

"I'm not getting a warning. But still . . ." Obi-Wan shook his head. The problem was the energy on this planet. Dark waves buffeted him from every side. It was like swimming in an evil sea. All that darkness made it hard to distinguish what was a true threat.

"It could just be a case of not wanting to be seen with us," Siri pointed out. "One of us should go in first to check it out."

"I'll go." Anakin and Ferus spoke the words together.

"I will." The words came from Ry-Gaul. He strode forward, pushed open the rusty metal door, and disappeared inside. No doubt Ry-Gaul's height and size would serve to deter anyone who wanted to challenge him.

The rest of them waited, every second wearing on their nerves. Finally Ry-Gaul emerged and said, "He's there. All clear."

They followed Ry-Gaul into the café. Apparently the sagging roof scared off customers, for only one man sat inside, at a table near the door. He hugged a mug with one hand and kept his eyes darting from the door to the roof, as if expecting it to crash down at any moment.

Teluron Thacker was a tall humanoid with pale skin and the soft look of a being used to spending time indoors, sitting down. He greeted the Jedi with a nervous nod and drew his red cape around his body.

"Thank you for seeing us," Obi-Wan said.

"The Jedi helped my home world of Eeyyon," Thacker said. "I pledged to help whenever I could."

"How do you find yourself on Korriban?" Siri asked.

"Just lucky I guess," Thacker groaned. "I angered my boss. Such a little thing, but she was so touchy. So I didn't check references and the deal went bad. What's a few million credits? The next thing I know, I get handed an assignment to open an office on Korriban." Thacker shuddered. "I haven't slept through the night since."

Obi-Wan signaled to the bartender to bring a round of drinks. In such a place, it was better to place an order, even though he wouldn't touch anything they were pouring. He waited until the bartender slammed down a pot of grog that slopped over the rim, then dropped a pile of not-too clean mugs onto the table.

Thacker leaned over and whispered. "I wouldn't drink that if I were you."

"Thanks for the tip," Siri said. "What can you tell us about the two beings we're pursuing?"

"Only that they are here," Thacker said. "A human man and woman have been seen. They match the descriptions perfectly. I checked the one hotel and several guest houses, and they aren't registered."

"They wouldn't use their real names," Obi-Wan said. "Did you give descriptions?"

"Well, I said a man and a woman, traveling together," Thacker said.

"Did you try anything else? Is there a database for arrivals and departures?"

Thacker shook his head. "Nobody really keeps track."

"Have you looked into whether any businesses here are a cover for Omega's enterprises?" Obi-Wan asked.

"Well, no," Thacker said. "Naturally I want to help the Jedi. But it is not wise to ask too many questions on Korriban."

"Why?" This question came from Ry-Gaul, and it stopped Thacker in his tracks.

"Uh, because." Thacker shrugged. "Because that's what everyone says."

Obi-Wan exchanged an exasperated glance with Siri. It was clear that Thacker wasn't going to be much help. He was too intimidated by even the rumor of possible problems.

"I should warn you about something. You know that the Commerce Guild has its own army? Well, there's a division here," Thacker said. "They say it's out of necessity, to protect the business workers from petty crime. But spider and surveillance droids are everywhere. If Omega and Zan Arbor have any contacts in the Commerce Guild, they could have access to all the surveillance information. Which means they could see everything."

At last, a piece of information they could use. But what else could Thacker tell them? Obi-Wan didn't want to leave the café without a solid lead. Then a thought occurred to him.

"Zan Arbor has expensive tastes," he said. "She is most likely not too thrilled to be here. There doesn't seem to be much luxury in Dreshdae."

"It's a stinking rot," Thacker agreed.

"Yet there are business executives here, creatures used to having the best of everything," Obi-Wan said. "There must be something for them. If you're looking to buy special items, where would you go?"

"There's a loose kind of black market," Thacker told them. "Run by thieves, of course. Supplies are low, there are no stores, and it's hard to even find essentials, like blankets or thermal capes, even though this dump of a rotting death-hole freezes your bones. They rob when they can — from the better buildings, the offices. No hotel room in the spaceport is safe. They've made some hits on ships coming in with supplies for the Commerce Guild executives."

"So how do you get in touch with this black market?" Obi-Wan asked.

"It's on the outskirts, in a plaza that's in ruins — that is, if you can tell ruins from the rest of these crumbling, cracked-up excuses for buildings." Thacker's darting gaze flicked to the ceiling. "I can give you the coordinates. If you want something, go at dusk. Ask for Auben. She's the best of a bad lot — she won't cheat you and she knows everything that's going on. I've bought a few things from her myself. But watch out for the army — the executives in the Commerce Guild are tired of buying back their own items. They want to smash the black market."

The Jedi stood.

"One more thing," Thacker said. "The army isn't your only concern. Auben might be less than cooperative. She won't trust you. And she's heavily armed."

"That won't be a problem," Obi-Wan assured him.

CHAPTER SEVEN

Dusk on Korriban lasted for hours, beginning in mid-afternoon as the weak sun slowly made its descent. The shadows cast by the buildings on Dreshdae seemed thick and full of menace. There had been an attempt to install glow lights on the streets, but they were staggered in odd patterns. As the Jedi walked toward the plaza, they moved from light to shadow. They knew it was dusk only because the light was failing. There was so much cloud cover that they could not see the sun. The clouds just deepened to a dark red.

"I have a suggestion, Master," Anakin said. "This Auben might feel less threatened if she's approached by one person. Especially someone young."

Obi-Wan nodded. "That's not a bad idea."

"We can't surround her, we'll spook her for sure," Siri said. "Why don't Anakin and Ferus go?"

Obi-Wan nodded. "You can say that you're brothers, and you've been stranded here. Sounds plausible."

Brothers! Anakin swallowed his groan. Being teamed with Ferus was bad enough.

They approached the plaza. It was surrounded by pillars that had once held up some sort of roof over the plaza. Part of the roof still hung over the space. Behind the pillars were the ruins of a building. There were plenty of places to hide, which was no doubt why it was chosen as the spot to conduct illegal business.

"We'll stay here," Obi-Wan said, stopping a good distance away from the plaza. "Whatever you do, don't reveal that you are Jedi. That's information that can be sold. We know Omega is expecting us, but he doesn't know when we'll arrive."

Anakin and Ferus took off for the marketplace in silence. The tension hadn't lessened between them. Anakin had hoped to gain information about Omega before Ferus did. He wished he were meeting Auben alone. It wasn't that he would jeopardize the mission in any way, but he wouldn't mind being one half-step ahead.

They didn't say a word as they walked. They didn't make a plan. Anakin wanted to complete the assignment as quickly as possible and return to the others.

They cruised once around the plaza. They could see a few beings in the shadows. It wasn't until they'd made one circuit of the area that they were approached.

A young woman dressed in a tight-fitting gray tunic and leggings came to them. She wore a leather headpiece that fitted snugly over her ears, and she carried an enormous satchel on her back without strain.

"Looking for something, friends?"

"Are you Auben?" Anakin asked.

Her eyes flicked over them. "Who wants to know?"

"Thacker sent us. He said you had things for sale."

"I've got it or I can get it. What's your need, friend?"

"Blankets and handwarmers," Anakin said.

She dumped the satchel on the ground and held up two handwarmers. As she crouched, Anakin saw two blasters in her belt. "Let me see the credits first," she said.

Anakin held out his hand. She took the credits from it, then tossed the handwarmers to Ferus. "No blankets today, but I've got a tip on some plush thermal capes. You can meet me here same time tomorrow and I'll have them."

"How much?" Ferus asked.

Auben named the price. Ferus raised his eyebrows.

"I said they were plush. Top quality. I'll have some

other luxury stuff, too." She shrugged. "If you don't want them, someone else will."

"You have a lot of customers?" Ferus's gaze roamed the empty plaza, pretending skepticism.

"I've got the whole spaceport as customers, friend." Auben shrugged the pack back onto her shoulders.

It was clear she was about to take off. Anakin spoke quickly. "Our parents marooned us here on Dreshdae. They said they'd be back, but it's been a few weeks now, and we don't know where —"

Auben's face was expressionless. "I don't need your story, just your credits."

"We heard that a couple landed at the spaceport recently," Anakin continued. "A human man and woman. Maybe you've seen them —"

Auben's eyes grew hard. "I don't discuss my customers."

"But I just —"

"Ever."

Anakin knew they were at a dead end.

"So you only find things, not beings?" Ferus asked. "Seems to me that there's not much difference. You need the same skills. Contacts and discretion."

She stopped in her tracks. "What do you mean?"

"It seems to me that for the right price, you could help us with more than handwarmers."

Auben hesitated. She gave them an appraising look, as if wondering how much they could pay.

But before she could speak, a blast of artillery fire shattered a column behind her. The explosion of rocks sent her flying toward Anakin and Ferus. All three landed on the ground.

"Commerce Guild droids," she panted. "Run!"

CHAPTER EIGHT

Auben took off. Anakin dashed after her. She had placed herself in an exposed position, her back to the blaster fire, thinking she could outrun it. She was wrong. Anakin had no choice. The Force slowed down time, and he could see the blaster bolts streaking toward her emanating from a phalanx of spider droids. He withdrew his lightsaber and leaped to deflect them.

He twisted in midair and landed on the top of a pillar, where he leaped again, this time next to Auben as he swept his lightsaber to deflect more fire.

"Who are you?" she yelled, but there was no time for Anakin to answer.

Ferus dashed forward, covering their retreat. Anakin hustled Auben into the shelter of the dark ruins. They paused a moment to catch their breath.

Auben looked at the lightsaber. "Where can I get one of those?"

Ferus ran in, already sheathing his lightsaber. "They have tracking droids. We've got to get out of here."

"We don't know which way," Anakin said to Auben.

She blew out a quick, exasperated breath, then nodded her head. "Okay, okay, seeing that you saved my life, I'll save yours. Come on."

She led the way through the ruins, twisting through narrow passageways and climbing through blasted-out holes. Anakin knew that the other Jedi were following them. He could feel them close.

The noise of the blaster fire faded, but Anakin knew the army hadn't given up. He could feel their presence, too. They were heading toward the outskirts of the spaceport now.

Auben led Anakin and Ferus out of the ruins and into a series of narrow, twisting streets. The street dwindled into a lane. The small hovels and buildings were spaced farther and farther apart until they were alone in a rocky landscape. The lane turned into a narrow dirt path that twisted and turned sharply upward. Anakin guessed that they were climbing the lip of the plateau that cradled the spaceport. Sure enough, they soon scrambled over a last obstacle of huge boulders and reached it.

Anakin looked down. Below them an ancient structure rose out of the steep mountainside and spilled out into a narrow valley. The mountain made two-thirds of the structure impenetrable. The entrance was in ruins, blocked by huge toppled columns and blocks of crumbling stone.

Anakin felt the peculiar stomach-turning wrench he experienced when faced with the tremors of the dark side of the Force. He knew what this wreck of a building was.

The ancient Sith monastery spread out below him, deserted for centuries, and still a presence of evil. Here was where thousands of Sith had once trained — and thousands of hopefuls had once disappeared forever.

"Is that where we're going?" Ferus asked.

"Creepy, huh? Don't let it bother you," Auben said. "Nobody lives there. Everyone's afraid to go inside, except for me. We won't be followed, that's for sure."

"What was it?" Ferus asked, even though Anakin knew he was perfectly aware of its history. Ferus was too good a student. He had read the same briefing material that Anakin had.

"Just an old monastery. They blasted out the side of the mountain to build it. Will you two hurry up?" Auben started down the steep path toward the monastery. It wound through the boulders and crags.

Something in Anakin suddenly revolted. He rarely felt fear, but he felt it now. A deep voice within him was warning him not to enter.

And yet another voice, deeper than fear, told him to go inside.

CHAPTER NINE

Obi-Wan lowered his electrobinoculars. "The Sith monastery," he said. "Why is she going there?"

"She doesn't want to be found," Soara answered. "I'd guess very few go in there if they don't have to."

They stood on the lip of the plateau, looking down. Thousands of standard years ago, the original inhabitants of Korriban had all been killed after toiling for years to build the monastery. Nothing living thrived there now. Not a bush, not a blade of grass. If the ancient stones could speak, they would talk of blood and terror.

"It could be a trap," Siri said.

"Every step we take on this planet could be leading us to a trap," Obi-Wan said.

Siri gave a half-smile. "So let's go."

They climbed down the steep, rocky path. Through the electrobinoculars, Obi-Wan had seen Auben lead Anakin and Ferus into the monastery through a crevice in the stones. He led the team there. The rocks that made up the giant walls had shifted over the years. Some large slabs leaned against each other, while others had toppled and crumbled into boulders.

Darra and Tru slipped through the crevice easily. Siri, Soara, and Obi-Wan followed — Obi-Wan with a bit more difficulty. Ry-Gaul had the worst time. He was tall and solidly built, and even the Force couldn't get him through the crack. "I'll find another way in," he said when it was clear he couldn't make it.

"I'll come with you, Master," Tru said, starting to slither out again.

"No. I'll catch up." Ry-Gaul disappeared.

Obi-Wan went a few steps ahead into the darkness. He felt the dread of the place. They were in a vast chamber, as big as the Great Hall of the Temple. Massive blocks of stone formed the floor. The last of the light came through the crevices in the walls like bony fingers.

They heard footsteps echoing as Auben led Anakin and Ferus farther into the ruins. The Jedi followed silently. The oppressiveness of the place where Sith had lived and trained was a burden they had to fight against. Obi-Wan heard voices, but he knew they were ancient ones. He thought he saw shadows move. When he turned a corner quickly, he saw a vision — a Sith student on his knees, begging . . .

He averted his eyes.

Siri's face was pale. Darra and Tru looked shaken. Soara moved closer to her apprentice, to give her support.

In the distance, Auben climbed through a ruined doorway. The Jedi moved to follow, keeping out of sight.

They stopped outside a small chamber. They could see through the half-ruined wall that this had once been a small enclosure, perhaps a reception room. Auben had turned it into a combination hideout and storage space. Along the walls were bins filled with what Obi-Wan had no doubt were stolen goods. There was a bedroll in the corner and a couple of durasteel boxes stacked to form a table. On it rested a glow lamp. Auben leaned over and switched it onto a low setting. Shadows sprang up, dark and ominous, as if the Sith hopefuls who had trained here had returned.

Auben turned to face Anakin and Ferus, her hands on her hips. "So. Who are you really?" Her voice echoed against the walls.

"We told you," Anakin said. "We're stranded."

"I think you are Jedi," Auben said. "I've never seen

a Jedi, but I've heard of them." She waited, but Ferus and Anakin did not speak. She shrugged. "Fine. Jedi credits are as good as anyone else's, I guess. If you wait a little while, the army will stop tracking and you can leave. They won't come inside the monastery."

"Do you live here alone?" Ferus asked.

Auben leaned toward the light as though it would give heat as well as illumination. "I live many places. But yes, I'm alone here. Sometimes I get spooked. I hear things . . . but it's just this old place."

"Maybe we should look around for you," Ferus said. "Make sure you're safe."

"I don't need any help," Auben said. "I have my friends to help me." She patted her belt, where her two blaster pistols were. "So, tell me. Are you really looking for a man and woman? And don't tell me they're your parents."

"Yes, we're looking for a couple," Ferus admitted.

"Do you think you can help us?" Anakin asked.

Auben crossed her arms. "If you're Jedi, you can make it worth my while, right? I hear the Jedi control a vast fortune."

"Who says that?" Ferus asked sharply.

She shrugged. "It's just what they say."

"Well, it's not true," Anakin said. "But we can make it worth your while, anyway. Do you know something?"

Auben was in the middle of her usual evasive shrug when an explosive blast rocked the walls. Sand spilled from the ceiling. Auben was almost knocked to the floor. Anakin and Ferus rose.

Behind the wall, Obi-Wan and the Jedi team ducked with the explosion, keeping their balance with difficulty.

Suddenly they heard the sound of pounding footsteps and the unmistakable *clack clack* of spider droids snapping into attack position.

Auben had been wrong. The Commerce Guild army had followed them.

Inside the chamber, Auben jumped up, blasters already gripped in her hands. "They're coming through the main chamber. There's only one other way out. Follow me."

Obi-Wan waited until he saw Auben kick open a small opening in the wall. He leaned over to Tru and Darra. "Stay with Anakin and Ferus, whatever happens. We'll take care of the droids and come find you."

Darra and Tru nodded. Quickly, they slipped into the now empty chamber and followed the others.

Obi-Wan, Siri, and Soara charged back to the main chamber, prepared to meet an army.

CHAPTER TEN

Anakin wasn't about to let Auben out of his sight. He had a feeling she was the key to finding Granta Omega. She knew so much about Dreshdae, and there was something in her eyes when they told her they were looking for a couple. His instincts told him she knew something.

Unfortunately, Ferus felt it, too.

Anakin could feel Ferus behind him every step of the way. They were moving close together in the narrow passage, Ferus's breath on his neck.

As Auben pushed forward, he realized that they were now moving parallel to the great hall. Despite the thick blocks of stone, he could hear the clatter of droids and the steady, fast ping of blaster fire.

Auben moved more quickly as the noise of the

blaster fire faded, no longer afraid of being detected. The passageway led downward in a gradual slope. The stones were damp and slippery.

"Where are we going?" Ferus asked.

"Just follow me," Auben snapped. "And hurry!"

The passageway made a sudden turn, and they came to a partially demolished wall. Auben stepped over the stones and jumped into a chamber a little larger than the one they left.

"There's a whole system of passageways that were once hidden," she explained. "I guess the big monks used to spy on the rest."

That sounded like standard Sith procedure to Anakin. Trust was not part of Sith doctrine. It seemed to Anakin to be a bleak way to live.

Auben led them down a bigger hallway. They went steadily downward, deeper and deeper into the complex. The walls began to weep with moisture. Anakin guessed they were now in the part of the monastery buried in the mountain.

They went through so many twists and turns that Anakin wondered if they'd have to use tracking devices to get out again. Even with his Jedi memory skills, he was beginning to feel disoriented.

At last, Auben paused. "What I'm about to show you isn't visible from above." She pushed open a rotted door.

Anakin followed. An ancient ship stood in the middle of a large space. He had never seen anything like it. Crude and clunky, it must have been state-of-the-art at one time. The afterburner tanks were huge.

"This was probably from before the sublight engine was perfected," Anakin said, half to himself. Under normal circumstances, he would love to investigate the ancient technology of the ship.

Around it, various decaying parts of what looked like droids were littered, models so old he couldn't identify them. He saw sheets and shards of durasteel and other metals on the floor and realized they had once been servodrivers, valves, and pumps, the hoses long decayed.

"It's a service bay," he said. "We must be near a landing hangar."

"You got it," Auben said. "Look."

She led them through the open arch, into the darkness. Anakin stepped out and released a breath. The hangar was so vast, it ended in darkness. Service bay after service bay ran down each side of the hangar, waiting to repair the ships that no longer arrived. Hulking wrecks of ships still littered the floor, bits of metal that had once been droids, decayed tanks. Huge statues of terrifying creatures from many worlds marched on either side down the hangar. The statues had crumbled and cracked over the years. Some were headless, and the huge heads had fallen and crumbled into blocks of stone.

There was a smell of rust and rot, and the air seemed full of something thick, something like memory. Here the Sith had sent off their attack ships. Here their blood lust had pooled into technology and aggression. Here they had thought themselves invincible. Here disaster had overtaken them, their vengeance ending in defeat as their greed tore their order apart.

"It's huge," Ferus said. He walked forward a few steps. "You could dispatch an army from here."

"Yeah, a lot of ships for a bunch of monks," Auben said.

"The Sith were more than monks," Anakin told her.

"So I've heard. The original evil guys, right?" Auben looked around. "Well, they're all dead now."

All except for one, Anakin thought. *Maybe two.* If Auben knew as much as they did about the Sith, she wouldn't be so casual.

"So where's the exit?" Ferus asked.

Auben waved vaguely toward the darkness. "The landing platform is completely blocked off. From what I can tell, it's buried behind the mountain again, probably blasted with artillery a couple of thousand years ago or so. But you can get out through one of the hangar bays.

It's a tough climb down the mountain, but it's better than tangling with the army."

Anakin suddenly felt a surge, a feeling that seemed to rise up through the soles of his feet and blast out the ends of his hair. His stomach turned. His nerves screamed an alert. He could feel the dark side of the Force, lurking deeply in the vast hangar.

"Anakin," Ferus said softly.

"I know."

"Let's . . . go back. Quietly."

They backed up, stepping into the service bay again. The cool shadow calmed Anakin's tripping heart.

Auben looked at both of them. "What is it?"

"Something worse than the army," Anakin said. "And it's coming this way."

CHAPTER ELEVEN

Obi-Wan quickly assessed the attack. The first and second lines were made up of dwarf spider droids and homing spider droids, skittering toward the Jedi with laser tracking devices sending thin blue lines bisecting the space between them. Behind the droids were the army troops, locals dressed in full plastoid armor with battlefield helmets. The sophistication of the force was surprising. Obi-Wan wondered why the Commerce Guild needed such an awesome security operation.

The blaster fire from the spider droids was fast and accurate. They marched on spindly legs toward the Jedi. Obi-Wan and Siri moved forward, lightsabers moving like pinwheels of glowing light, cutting down the first droids who moved forward to engage them.

They had fought together so many times that they

had learned how to merge their styles. Siri was the flash, Obi-Wan the strategist. He set her up, and she closed the deal. He maneuvered, she struck. They moved faster than the droids could track, and, with Soara entering from the other side, they mowed down the first two lines easily.

Soara was a renowned fighter, and Obi-Wan always appreciated a chance to watch her technique. She was a fluid force, moving like wind and water. Each stroke of her lightsaber was calculated, yet there seemed to be no calculation in her style. There was only movement. She took out five droids with one steady arc, knocking off their heads and sending the metal clanging to the stone floor.

Smoke filled the air and drifted to the vast space above. Deflected blaster bolts shot back at the startled officers, who found it hard to hold their line. They soon realized that they were not dealing with straggly thieves with a few blasters in their belts. They grabbed blaster rifles off the holsters strapped to their backs and fired. Two dozen of them advanced, while the third wave of droids moved in. Obi-Wan began to break into a sweat. He did not see the possibility of defeat, but the last thing he needed was to get clipped by blaster fire and have to deal with a wound while chasing Omega.

Then, from behind the officers, Ry-Gaul appeared

out of the shadows. His silver-gray lightsaber hummed as he held it straight for a moment in front of him, gauging what he was up against. He moved quickly for his size, rather like Qui-Gon had, his grace surprising while his great strength never flagged.

The officers who turned to engage him couldn't get away fast enough. The remaining squad took one look at three Jedi to the front and one to the rear and began to retreat, firing as they did so.

They let them go. The presence of Jedi on the planet couldn't stay a secret for very long. Jedi did not take a life if they didn't have to.

As soon as they were safe, Obi-Wan whipped out his comlink. He couldn't reach Anakin. Siri tried as well, then shook her head.

"Too much interference here," she said. "We'll have to find them."

Obi-Wan felt something then. A flicker that started on the edges of his consciousness and then grew, a dark shape inside him.

He spoke quietly despite the dread in his heart. "He's here."

The others turned to him. "Who?" Siri asked.

"The Sith. He's here, in the monastery. Somewhere."

Then he saw the knowledge flash in Siri's face, Soara's posture, Ry-Gaul's wintry eyes.

They looked at each other for a moment, deep worry now ticking inside them.

A Sith was here, and their Padawans were by themselves.

CHAPTER TWELVE

Anakin heard the flurry. It was like a flock of birds. But instead of the whisper of feathers, he heard the mechanical clatter of metal on stone.

"Stay here," Ferus ordered Auben. "And hide!" he yelled over his shoulder.

Together Ferus and Anakin moved to the front of the service bay. They peered out into the vast hangar. At first they could see nothing. They could hear only the menacing clatter.

Then out of the gloom rose the battle droids. Line after line. Maybe thirty . . . forty?

"Wait," Ferus said. "Those aren't ordinary battle droids."

"They have reinforced armor," Anakin said, swallowing. "And the control center is lower . . . you can't cut off their heads."

"Too many," Ferus said. "We have to retreat."

"We can take them," Anakin insisted.

"Anakin, this is no time to play hero. The two of us can't do it by ourselves."

"That's your trouble, Ferus," Anakin said coolly. "You always look at the odds."

He stepped out into the darkness of the hangar. He saw the infrared tracking devices on the droids move over the space. They would find him. He had seconds.

Ferus moved out next to him. Of course if Anakin went out to meet the droids, Ferus would have to as well. He wouldn't leave him. Anakin knew that.

"We should attack from above. They won't be expecting that," he said.

"How —"

"Follow me."

Anakin gathered in the Force. He leaped onto the gigantic statue to his left, landing on its knee. He began to climb rapidly up, looking for handholds in the crumbling stone. He heard Ferus behind him.

He balanced on one shoulder of the huge statue, Ferus on another. They were high above the floor now, but even so, the ceiling of the hangar was lost in the darkness above them.

"Wait for the first wave, then drop," Anakin said. "We can use our liquid cable launchers. The statues can be cover and —"

"I get it," Ferus said.

They waited for the precise instant their attack would be most effective. It was seconds away when two dark shapes ran out from the hangar.

Darra and Tru.

"They think we're down there," Ferus said in horror.

Almost immediately, the droids locked onto Darra and Tru's positions.

Ferus and Anakin took off in midair, the liquid cables holding them secure. They bounced off the statue and then swung out over the first line of droids. Their lightsabers moved in slashing circles. Due to the unexpected angle of attack, the droids were unable to lock onto their position at first. Sweeping out over the line, they managed to take out a dozen droids between them. Racing forward, Darra and Tru engaged the rest.

The eerie space and the darkness, the glint of metal, the pull of battle. Anakin saw nothing, felt nothing, but what was before him. He wasn't a fool. He knew their chances of beating so many droids were slim to none. But he also knew that it was only in gestures like this that a true Jedi would be revealed. He Force-pushed a droid and it slammed into another. He slashed them both into one smoking pile.

Compared to him, Ferus's hold on the Force was puny. Anakin reached out for it in the way he knew, reached for the Force in the stones and the dust and very air he breathed. The Force was part of him and around him. His vision was sharper now, his control perfect. He didn't count the droids he dismantled. He didn't hesitate or second-guess his choices. He just kept moving.

Even while he moved, he kept track of the Padawans behind him and next to him. In battle, his problems with Ferus went away. They were fellow Jedi, and they had to cover one another.

The droids split off in a different formation. Darra, who had swung wide to attack, was suddenly surrounded. She whirled in an arc, keeping most of them at bay. Tru, who was closest, Force-leaped to help her, his flexible arms reaching out to slash his way toward her. Darra buried her lightsaber in the lead droid's control panel and it wheeled crazily astray, spraying blaster fire in random, dizzying circles. The stray fire caught Tru in mid-leap. He was wounded and fell, his lightsaber clattering to the floor. A droid stepped on it and kept going.

Anakin started to rush to help, but out of the corner of his eye he saw a flicker of movement. Something sinuous, flowing. Not the movement of a droid.

A cape. A dark-robed figure was moving quickly, keeping in the shadows, heading into the shadowy end of the hangar.

Granta Omega.

Tru was down. Darra had leaped to protect him. Now Ferus was moving in that direction.

The situation was covered. And Omega was getting away, no doubt heading for the same exit that Auben had told them about. This was his chance, his only chance. With a last glance at his friend, Anakin ran off into the darkness.

CHAPTER THIRTEEN

Ry-Gaul led the way. "When I couldn't get in, I followed the wall back into the mountain. There's an old landing hangar. It's enormous — maybe a hundred service bays on each side. I got In through one of the end bays. That's where they are."

"The Padawans won't know it's a Sith," Soara said. "Until . . ."

They all finished the sentence in their minds.

Until it's too late.

Ry-Gaul led them steadily downward. Obi-Wan could feel the mountain as if it were pressing on his back. The closer they got, the more dread he felt.

They were deep in the monastery now. Even though it was in ruins, Obi-Wan could see how different it was from the Jedi Temple. Although the Sith monastery had the same goals — study and training — it was clear that this had been a place ruled by fear. The Temple had grand rooms, but it also had quiet spaces, light-filled classrooms, gardens. The Jedi believed that beauty was a part of the Force, and encouraged it. The sound of water, the play of light, the grace of a curving stairway — the Temple had been planned as a place of comfort as well as rigor.

The lines of this place were harsh. The walls were high, but narrowed slightly as they rose, in order to create a sense of being trapped. Angles were slightly off in a way that Obi-Wan realized was deliberate. The monastery was designed to intimidate, to keep beings off-balance. There were no openings to air or light. There was only cold gray stone, massive columns, hard floors. Amid the weeping stones, Obi-Wan could still feel the fear that had ruled there, the many beings who had come to learn evil, the ones who had come naively, hoping for some kind of enlightenment, and had been trapped by their own desires.

He shuddered. It was as though he could feel each wasted life. Each terrible death.

The rest of the Jedi were silent. He knew they felt it, too.

At last Ry-Gaul stepped through a doorway into what had once been a service bay. They saw Auben cowering behind the wreck of an ancient vehicle. Wordlessly, she pointed to the curved arch that led to the hangar.

It was the silence that frightened them. They rushed out into the hangar.

It was littered with the remains of droids — so many that Obi-Wan staggered. Had the Padawans destroyed them all?

They could see that the battle had just ended seconds before. Tru lay on the ground. Ferus leaned over him, tending a wound with bacta. Darra whirled around and saw them, her lightsaber still activated. She shut it down as Ry-Gaul moved toward his wounded Padawan with his usual efficient speed.

Fear welled up in Obi-Wan.

Where is Anakin?

Darra saw the question in his eyes. "He ran that way — I think he saw something." She pointed to the darkness at the end of the vast hangar.

Obi-Wan started to run. He would have to rely on the Force to find Anakin. He opened himself up to it, hoping it would reveal to him what he needed to know. Was his Padawan wounded? Had the worst happened?

He had no doubt what Anakin was chasing. No matter what Anakin thought, he was not equipped to deal with a Sith.

Obi-Wan ran into the darkness. He could not risk a

light, not even his lightsaber. The darkness seemed to invade his lungs, making it hard for him to breathe. He scrambled over fallen blocks of stone, engine parts, the shreds of machines and the skeletons of vehicles. It was difficult to keep his footing but he made no sound.

He saw movement ahead and realized he had found Anakin. Relief flooded him, rendering him weak for a moment. He had been so afraid, and now he wondered momentarily at his fear. It seemed out of proportion to what he knew of Anakin's skills. All he knew was that he had an overwhelming need to protect his Padawan from the Sith, to stand between Anakin and the dark side. Natural, he supposed.

Anakin was moving quickly, hugging the wall of the hangar. His focus was so intent that he did not sense Obi-Wan behind him. Obi-Wan noted this with alarm. How many times had he warned Anakin to never focus on the goal ahead only, but to cast his attention like a net, as far around him as he could? He should have sensed his Master. Obi-Wan quickened his pace. He felt the dark side of the Force grow and gather, and he wanted to call out to Anakin, but didn't want to give away their positions.

He needn't have worried. Whoever the Sith was, he knew exactly where Anakin was, for, to Obi-Wan's horror, his apprentice was suddenly lifted like a doll and flung into the air. Anakin's body slammed into the wreck of a cruiser. He fell to the ground.

Obi-Wan raced forward, his lightsaber activated and ready for battle. He kept his focus wide, just as he had taught Anakin. He knew the Sith was aware that he was there, and no doubt was aware that he would rush to help his apprentice.

No attack came. Anakin was already recovering as Obi-Wan bent over him, quickly checking for breaks or contusions.

"I'm all right." Anakin grunted. "Just . . . embarrassed. I've never felt anything like that."

"Did you see him?"

"Only from behind. Tall. Dressed in a black-hooded cape that trailed all the way to the ground. I didn't see his face. He didn't even turn. I felt the Force come at me like an autoblaster cannon. . . ." Anakin struggled to his feet. "It could be a Sith."

"I know."

Anakin started forward.

"Where are you going?" Obi-Wan asked.

When he turned, Obi-Wan could see Anakin's face undergo a change. Every muscle tightened, and his eyes turned flinty.

"We have a chance to make a stand," Anakin said.

"We need the others."

"It will be too late."

Obi-Wan hesitated only a fraction. Anakin was right. They had to try. He started forward, and together they moved farther into the darkness.

"Keep your focus loose," Obi-Wan warned him in a low tone. "He will come from anywhere when he comes."

"This time I'll be prepared."

"Don't be so confident," Obi-Wan answered. "You probably won't be."

They were nearing the end of the hangar. He sensed it rather than saw it. The corroded vehicles were more numerous now, lined up like dark, giant phantoms.

Like phantoms . . .

Phantoms that move . . .

Obi-Wan wrenched his gaze away. He could have sworn the ancient ships were moving.

Then he knew.

"This way!" he yelled, as the first vehicle suddenly flipped over. It would have crushed them if Obi-Wan hadn't dashed to the side with Anakin on his heels. He flattened himself against the wall as another vehicle moved, its jagged wing a lethal weapon, capable of slicing them to ribbons. A cruiser suddenly zoomed toward the wall, straight at them.

"Drop!" Anakin and Obi-Wan hit the floor, hugging the stones as the cruiser passed over them and smashed into the wall.

Vehicle parts began to fall like rain. The crashes were deafening. They leaped, twisted, and dived to avoid them, using the Force to deflect them when they could. Finally they came to rest in the shadow of one of the giant statues. Obi-Wan leaned against a clawed foot and squinted into the darkness.

He could not see the Sith, but he felt the Sith's amusement, his triumph.

The vehicles now smashed into one another, creating a solid mass of screaming metal, effectively blocking them from the front of the hangar.

Anakin ran to the mountain of metal and tried to climb over it. Obi-Wan felt the dark side rise in a crest and then fall, leaving a vacuum behind.

"It's no use," he told Anakin. "The Sith is gone."

"Gone." Anakin repeated the word dully.

"Don't worry." Obi-Wan sheathed his lightsaber. "I have no doubt that we'll meet him again."

CHAPTER FOURTEEN

Anakin immediately hurried to Tru's side while Obi-Wan went to confer with the Masters.

"You all right?"

Tru smiled wanly, but didn't look up. "Just a few bruises. Ferus fixed me up."

Ferus tucked the med kit back into his utility pouch. He didn't look at Anakin, either. Darra studied the hilt of her lightsaber.

"I saw someone trying to escape, so I had to go after him," Anakin said. "It turned out to be a Sith. Obi-Wan is sure of it."

"Well, that's not surprising," Darra said. "We're on Korriban, after all."

There was an unfamiliar hard note in Darra's voice, as if she resented Anakin.

74

"Our mission is to find Granta Omega," Anakin said. "You had things under control, so I went after him — or, who I thought was him."

"So you were sure we had everything under control?" Ferus straightened, wiping his hands on his tunic.

"That's what I said."

"Tru was wounded, I was helping him, and Darra had to face off against a dozen droids, but everything was under control?"

"Obviously I made the right call," Anakin said, gesturing at the fallen droids.

"And you were only thinking of the mission, of course," Ferus said.

"Of course." Anakin knew what Ferus was getting at. He felt his neck heat up, and he turned away before the flush could reach his cheeks and betray him. The truth was less certain than his words. He was thinking of the mission, but he was also thinking of himself. He had been in a position to capture Omega without help. He had left Ferus behind with a secret satisfaction. He had wanted to win.

He sneaked a look back at Tru. His friend looked strained and unhappy. Anakin resolved to talk to him as soon as he could do so privately. Tru's friendship was very important to him. But Tru had to understand what was important to Anakin, too.

Anakin joined the Masters. Ry-Gaul and Soara were examining the battle droid wreckage.

"These are the super battle droids we've been hearing about," Soara said. "A complete violation of Republic regulations."

Obi-Wan looked grim. "We are lucky to all be standing. This could have been much worse. I think our next step is to trace the route of the Sith if we can. He most likely used the exit that you used to get inside, Ry-Gaul."

Ry-Gaul nodded. "That's why he blocked it."

"There's another possibility," Siri said. "The landing pad could be functional."

Anakin shook his head. "Auben said it's buried."

"So maybe it just looks buried," Siri said.

"Let's ask Auben," Anakin said. "She can show it to us, at least."

They walked inside the service bay. It was empty.

"She was hiding behind the old cruiser," Soara said. "Where could she have gone?"

"I doubt she'd return to the monastery," Ferus said. "She was afraid of the Commerce Guild army."

"She must have sneaked behind us when we were tending to Ferus," Siri said.

"Most likely heading for the other exit." Ferus swallowed. "She went toward the Sith."

The Jedi exchanged glances.

Without a word, they moved back to the dark front of the hangar. Using the Force, they searched each service bay as they ran, making sure Auben hadn't hid there. Finally they ended at the pile of vehicles and debris the Sith had used to block his escape. Grimly, they set to work with their lightsabers and cleared a smoking hole through the pileup. One by one, they crawled through.

They walked into the last bay on the line. A new cruiser stood there, its ramp down.

"Did you see this when you came in?" Obi-Wan asked Ry-Gaul.

He shook his head. "It must have landed after I left."

As they moved closer, they saw a body on the ramp. It was Auben.

She was dead.

CHAPTER FIFTEEN

Anakin rushed forward. He checked her vitals, even though he knew she was gone. "What happened?" he asked. "There's not a mark on her."

"Her heart just stopped beating," Siri said. "It's said that the Sith were capable of stopping a heart without even touching their victim."

"The question is, what was she doing here?" Obi-Wan asked.

Ferus had climbed up the ramp into the cruiser. He poked his head out. "That's easy to answer. Stealing." He held out two thermal capes. "She told Anakin and me that she could get her hands on some luxury goods."

"While you check out the ship, Darra and I will see if we can find the landing platform," Soara said.

Obi-Wan ran up the ramp. Quickly, he moved through the ship, searching for clues. It was evident that the ship had been left bare of everything except essentials or items that couldn't be traced. He quickly checked the nav computer. Even the archives were wiped.

"This is the Sith ship," he said.

"Expensive tastes," Ferus said, dropping the thermal capes with distaste.

"Auben must have found the ship sometime earlier," Obi-Wan guessed. "She wanted to nab some items on her way out."

"Never got the chance," Ferus said.

"Maybe," Obi-Wan murmured.

He started out of the cruiser. "Something I learned from Qui-Gon. When you catch a thief, he'll always pretend he was on his way *in,* not *out.*"

Anakin followed closely on Obi-Wan's heels. Obi-Wan bent over Auben. Gently, he reached underneath her body and withdrew her hand. He uncurled her fist.

"We just got lucky," he said. "The Sith was in a hurry. He didn't check."

"What is it?" Anakin asked.

"A holo-recorder," Obi-Wan said, holding it up. "One of the micro versions. She'd get a good price for it on the black market. And there's a received message here in the archive."

He pressed a button, and a miniature image of Granta Omega appeared.

Omega bowed. "Greetings, Master. We are grateful that our failure to complete our mission at the Senate did not disappoint you. As you generously said, the intent to disrupt and demoralize was achieved. The Senate is more divided than ever. It gratifies us that you have decided to entrust us with your secret. We have received the coordinates for our meeting. At last you will reveal yourself to us. We will then truly be able to further your cause throughout the galaxy." Omega bowed again. "Until we meet, I, Granta Omega, and Jenna Zan Arbor, servants to no one in the galaxy, remain servants to the Sith."

The hologram fragmented into a shimmer.

"Whew," Anakin said. "What a toadying dungcreeper."

"So they came here to meet the Sith, just as you thought," Siri said. "He's going to reveal his identity to them."

"Which means if we can find out where the meeting is, we'll find out as well," Obi-Wan said.

Siri pressed her lips together. "We have a whole planet to search."

A faraway look was in Obi-Wan's eyes. "No. There is only one possible place for them to meet," he said softly.

Soara and Darra appeared. "We found the landing platform," Soara said. "It's still completely functional. We found new access controls hidden in the ruins. Works like a charm. There's evidence of a recent take-off. By the looks of the scorch marks, I'd say it was a small airspeeder."

Obi-Wan looked back at Auben's body sprawled on the ramp. He tried to reconstruct what had happened. "He's been using this place as a hideout. He bumped into Auben — and he killed her. Then he left the cruiser and took the airspeeder. More maneuverable. Harder to track." And the airspeeder, Obi-Wan thought, would get him where he needed to go.

Obi-Wan felt a tug, as though a string had been tied to his breastbone. He walked down the ramp, across the remains of the hangar, and stood out on the landing platform Soara and Darra had found.

The chill wind knifed through his clothes as he stood outside. He was deep in the mountain. He could see the valley far below, and a vast expanse of gray sky.

He felt Omega. For the first time, he felt his energy. Though he wasn't a Sith, Omega had sought out the dark side of the Force. He had been unable to harness it for himself, but he had lived in it. Obi-Wan was tied to him, energy to energy. He could track him now without instruments. He didn't need clues, or tips.

"Master?" Anakin drifted to his side. "What is it?"

"I know where Omega is," Obi-Wan said. "He's in the Valley of the Dark Lords. And the Sith has gone to meet him there. We can uncover them both."

CHAPTER SIXTEEN

Obi-Wan contacted Jocasta Nu. They needed more information on the Valley of the Dark Lords. Superstition, legend, anything that could help give them an edge. The problem, of course, was that no one had dared to enter the valley for centuries. Or, at least, had lived to report on it.

Soara and Darra saw to Auben. They couldn't move her yet, so they wrapped her carefully in the thermal capes.

Anakin looked for Tru. He had disappeared, and so had Ferus. Feeling uneasy, Anakin headed off to see what they were up to. Would Ferus try to steal his best friend? He might fill Tru's mind with his version of why Anakin had left them to fight the droids alone. He would twist the facts to make Anakin look bad.

Tru and Ferus were sitting in one of the service bays, talking quietly. Ferus was busy working on Tru's lightsaber. Anakin paused in the shadows. Were they discussing him? He thought he heard his name. He concentrated fiercely.

"I noticed it," Ferus told Tru. "That droid must have pulverized your power circuit."

"It slips back into half-power without warning," Tru said in a worried voice.

Tru's lightsaber must have been damaged in the battle. But why hadn't Tru told Ry-Gaul? An apprentice was obligated to tell his or her Master if a lightsaber was damaged.

As if Tru had overheard Anakin's question, he said, "I know I should have told Ry-Gaul. But he's so correct. He might leave me out of battle situations, or even send me back to the Temple."

"If your lightsaber is permanently damaged, Ry-Gaul would be right to do so," Ferus said.

Typical, Anakin thought. Ferus always had to inform you of rules you knew by heart already.

"After all," Ferus continued, "you don't want to meet a Sith without a lightsaber."

"No kidding," Tru said. "This mission is crucial. That's why I can't be sent back. I just thought if I could fix it without having to tell Ry-Gaul . . ." Tru wound one flexible arm around his back to hug his opposite elbow, a gesture Anakin knew well. It was something Tru did when he was especially nervous. "Look, I know I wouldn't be the first or second candidate to enter the acceleration program — you and Anakin will be the first. Maybe Darra would be third. But I don't want to be left behind."

Ferus frowned. "Tru, your advancement is not the reason we're here."

"That's not what I mean!" Tru said, upset. "I want to stand with my fellow Jedi because we all know that the darkness is growing. We need every Jedi. I want to be there."

"We all do," Ferus said. He bent over the lightsaber, fine-tuning it. Anakin couldn't see what he was doing, but he was itching to get his own hands on the lightsaber. He was sure he was a better technician than Ferus.

"All right, I fixed it." Ferus put the handle back together and handed the lightsaber back to Tru. "You shouldn't have any more problems. Your power cell is boosted."

Anakin started to step forward. If Ferus had worked on the power cell, that meant that Tru needed to check the flux aperture again. Anakin had tweaked it before, but it might need an adjustment to compensate for the power boost. Anyway, it would be wise to double-check. Anakin had better tell him. But he stopped when he heard his name.

"Why didn't you ask Anakin to fix it?" Ferus asked. "He's better at this than I am."

"He was busy with Obi-Wan," Tru murmured.

Anakin realized that Tru had evaded the question. He could have asked him to help. He frowned as he watched the two Padawans, their heads close together.

Tru was drifting away from him. He could feel it.

Ferus stood. "I don't see any reason to tell Ry-Gaul, now that it's fixed. We'd better get back."

Angrily, Anakin retreated back into the shadows, then turned and headed for the others. He felt betrayed. Tru had chosen Ferus to confide in. He was Tru's best friend — he should have been the one to help him! Obviously, Tru was holding a grudge against him for not coming to his aid.

Well, if Tru didn't want his help, he certainly wasn't going to offer it. Most likely Ferus had done a perfect job. After all, he was almost a Jedi Knight.

What was strange, Anakin reflected, was that Ferus had agreed to keep Tru's secret. He would have expected Ferus to tell Ry-Gaul about the damaged lightsaber, or at least encourage Tru to do so. Instead, he had fixed it himself. Technically, it was a breach of the rules, and Ferus never broke the rules.

Anakin smiled. So the perfect Padawan wasn't so perfect after all.

He paused by the wreckage of the vehicles that the mysterious Sith had moved so easily. There was a disturbance in the air, as though the dark energy of the Force still pulsed around the wall of debris. As if the Sith had vanished, but left a pool of his darkness behind.

He felt something new inside him, but he couldn't put a name to it. He looked out into the grayness of the valley, just visible past the dark outlines of his Master and the other Jedi as they conferred on the landing platform. He concentrated hard. What was he feeling?

A beating heart. A being out there — somewhere — reaching out to him? It wasn't a connection . . . it was a call. It was something he didn't want, but something that drew him, pulled him. . . .

Granta Omega? Did he have the same connection

as his Master did? He didn't think so. Not this time. It didn't feel right. It felt . . . bigger. Hidden.

The Sith.

Anakin faced out to the valley. He felt the cold wind blow against his face. The Sith was calling him.

CHAPTER SEVENTEEN

Obi-Wan turned to the others. "We need to get to the cruisers. It's too far to hike to the valley. We only have about an hour of dusk left. We don't want to go in at night. Madame Nu gave me coordinates for the best approach."

Obi-Wan saw both relief and trepidation on the faces of the other Padawans. They all wanted to go. They wanted it and feared it.

He saw no fear on his Padawan's face, however. He wasn't sure how Anakin was feeling. There was something going on . . . underneath. Korriban had unsettled them all, Obi-Wan knew.

Even the Masters were not eager to enter the valley. They knew they were heading into great trouble. They knew there would be difficulty. Traps. Attacks. Surprises. The dark side of the Force could snare them, confuse them. But they each felt strongly that this was their only chance. The hidden darkness every Jedi felt was here. They could find it and expose it. End it. Here. Now.

Back at the Dreshdae landing platform, they hurried to their cruisers. Anakin sprang into the cockpit. He entered the coordinates Obi-Wan had given him for the Valley of the Dark Lords. They would have to find it through instruments, since it would not be visible. Then they would survey the area before deciding on a landing point.

Anakin did a preflight check, working quickly but carefully. All the indicator lights turned green. It was a go.

Except . . .

He tapped on an indicator. The light had shone green immediately. It should have cycled from orange to yellow first. Just a small thing, an indicator for the portside fuel baffles. If the light was red it would indicate a clogged baffle. Even that wouldn't prevent takeoff. He could fly with a clogged fuel baffle.

But why hadn't the indicator cycled through the colors?

"Problem?" Obi-Wan looked at him.

Anakin turned in the seat. The toolkit was clamped to the bottom of the counter. One of the clamps hadn't engaged all the way. It would rattle during turbulence. He would have noticed it on the flight here.

Someone had been aboard.

Through the windscreen, in the ship next to him, Ry-Gaul gave him a thumbs up.

"No!" Anakin shouted. He jumped forward and hit the comm. "Don't start the engines!"

Ry-Gaul looked at him, puzzled, and nodded.

"Anakin, what?" Obi-Wan asked, frowning at the urgent tone in Anakin's voice.

"Not sure yet." Anakin quickly disengaged the hatch and climbed down into the engine. He only a needed a few seconds before he saw it.

He vaulted out of the engine bloc. "We've got to get out. The other ship, too!"

Obi-Wan hit the comm. "Evacuate! Now!"

Anakin hit the ramp control at the same time. He, Ferus, Siri, and Obi-Wan charged down. They met Ry-Gaul, Tru, Darra, and Soara.

"Take cover!" Anakin shouted.

The Jedi raced to the opposite side of the landing platform and dived behind a cruiser as the two starships exploded in a fiery blast. They felt the heat on their faces. A wall of air hit them.

Slowly, Anakin rose. He regarded the skeletal frame of the starship with regret.

"That was one sweet cruiser," he said.

"What happened?" Siri asked.

"I saw an indicator light malfunction. It didn't cycle through."

"Which one?" Ry-Gaul asked.

"Fuel baffles. Then I noticed that someone had used the stowed toolkit. When I looked at the engine, I saw that someone had rigged the main reactor to blow on ignition. Then I noticed a small timer. I figured that after the preflight check if takeoff didn't take place, it would blow anyway."

"Well done," Ry-Gaul said.

"Very well done," Soara seconded, gazing at the burning ships.

"We're running out of time," Obi-Wan said. He took out his comlink.

"What are you going to do?" Anakin asked.

"I'm afraid that Teluron Thacker is going to find his courage."

"I doubt he'll want to give us a hand," Siri said.

"He doesn't have to give us a hand," Obi-Wan said. "Just a ship."

Within minutes, Thacker pulled into the landing platform in a large airspeeder with a bright orange shell. He looked at the smoking hulks of the cruisers.

He shuddered. "I'm not going to ask."

"Thanks for this," Obi-Wan said as Thacker quickly hopped out of the vehicle.

"It's the company airspeeder. For clients." Thacker looked worriedly at the smoking cruisers. "I'm not supposed to lend it out."

"We'll take good care of it," Obi-Wan said.

Anakin looked at the large speeder with disgust. "This will be like driving a gravsled." He knocked on the decorative fins on the outside. "A gooped-up gravsled, at that."

"It will fit all of us and it will get us there," Obi-Wan said. "Drive."

The Jedi climbed into the airspeeder. Thacker remained outside, watching them.

"At least it has a couple of sniper blasters," Anakin said approvingly as he surveyed the instrument panel. "They might come in handy."

"You've been a friend to the Jedi," Obi-Wan told Thacker. "We won't forget it."

Thacker swallowed. "I'm sorry."

"About what?" Obi-Wan said as Anakin powered up the engine.

"It isn't very fast, or agile . . ."

"It's all right."

"I'm sorry!" Thacker yelled as they took off.

"Jumpy fellow," Siri said, settling into her seat.

"Everyone's jumpy on Korriban," Darra said. "Can you blame them?"

Anakin guided the airspeeder high above Dreshdae. He entered the coordinates into the computer. "Estimated arrival in ten minutes," he said, pushing to the maximum speed.

Siri twisted around. "Hey, looks like security cruisers on our tail."

Suddenly, the comm unit crackled on the emergency channel.

"Attention, Koro-1 Deluxe Airspeeder. Land and show documentation. Stolen vehicle check. This is the Commerce Guild Army Patrol."

Obi-Wan pressed the transmission button. "Correction. Owner loaned the vehicle. Please check with owner Teluron Thacker."

"Negative. Owner Teluron Thacker reported vehicle stolen. Land or undergo firepower from laser cannon."

"Thacker betrayed us," Obi-Wan told the others. "That's why he was so jumpy. Somebody got to him."

"Someone he's more afraid of than the Jedi," Soara said. "Anakin, can you outfly those security vehicles?"

"Thirty seconds to land," the comm unit thundered.

"In this bucket?" Anakin gripped the controls. "If I have to."

"Then do it," Obi-Wan said.

"Hold on."

The words had barely left Anakin's lips when the Jedi were nearly plastered to the cockpit canopy as the ship went into a screeching dive. The army speeders struggled to keep up.

A blast from a laser cannon thundered by, shaking the ship. Anakin put the ship into a tight turn.

"Come on, come on," he muttered. "You can do it."

The second blast was closer.

"Use those sniper blasters," Obi-Wan directed. "If we give them some firepower they might back off. Just don't hit anything."

Anakin flipped on the sniper blaster controls. "They've been disabled."

Obi-Wan groaned. "Great."

"We've got to outrun them, then," Siri said.

"Head for the monastery," Ry-Gaul suggested. "The canyons will give you cover."

Anakin pushed the speeder into a climb that slammed them back into their seats. He tried a corkscrew turn, a movement that he could make with his eyes closed in a decent speeder. This one groaned with the effort. The controls shook in his hands as blaster bolts skittered across the hull.

"This isn't going to work," he muttered. "Ry-Gaul, can you take over?"

Ry-Gaul quickly slid into the pilot seat and Anakin transferred the controls. He crawled past the others to the rear.

"What are you doing?" Obi-Wan asked.

"If I can reduce the air drag, it can go faster." He spoke to Soara, who sat near a small toolkit built into the cabin wall. "Hand me that fusioncutter, will you? It's going to get windy," Anakin warned, before flipping open the canopy.

The wind whipped through the cabin. Anakin used a servodriver to disengage the canopy completely. It flew off the airspeeder, smacking the first security speeder straight in its windscreen. The blow sent the cruiser careening downward to the planet's surface.

"That was lucky," Anakin muttered.

He crawled out on the airspeeder. Buffeted by air currents and hanging on for his life whenever Ry-Gaul swerved to avoid cannonfire, Anakin crawled to the port fins. Using the fusioncutter, he sliced through the fastenings and kicked off the decorative fins. Laser bolts made the hair on the back of his neck stand at attention as the charge shuddered through the air. Anakin held on with his knees as he made deep cuts in the bright plastoid shell and kicked it off into space.

He crawled back inside the speeder. "Better?" he asked Ry-Gaul.

"Better. I can get it up past maximum speed."

To Anakin's surprise, Ry-Gaul inclined his head toward the controls, even as he made a hard left and went into a dive. "Take over."

Feeling pleased, Anakin slipped back into the pilot seat. A Jedi Master had passed the controls to him! Ry-Gaul was renowned as a pilot, and he thought Anakin better able to handle the evasive flying. Take that, Ferus!

Anakin kept pushing the speed. Even when the mountains loomed ahead, he didn't slow down. The airspeeder screamed down into the valley. He looped around a peak and dived into a canyon dotted with boulders. The three remaining army security speeders followed.

Anakin kept the craft close to the ground. This kind of flying came naturally to him. After all, he'd trained on Podracers.

He whipped through the canyon as if it were a racing course. He flew over boulders, squeezed through natural formations, sensing obstacles before they appeared. One speeder behind him clipped a wing and spun out of control.

"Another one down," Obi-Wan said. Anakin allowed himself a moment to look at his Master. He always enjoyed making Obi-Wan pale.

A tall formation grew out of the canyon floor. Anakin headed straight for it.

"Anakin, you're pushing it —"

"That's the idea."

"This speeder doesn't have that kind of maneuverability —"

"I guess we'll find out."

At the last possible second, Anakin wrenched the controls. Instead of turning, he went straight up. The bottom of the airspeeder skidded along the formation. The sound of screaming metal blocked out the sound of the engine. Smoke rose around them. Obi-Wan saw licks of flame on the airspeeder's body. He closed his eyes.

The security speeder behind them tried the same maneuver and crashed head-on into the rock. The second veered off, only to clip a wing. The wing dragged on the canyon floor, slowing the craft until it ground to a halt.

Anakin kept going straight up. When he was high

above the surface, he straightened out the airspeeder. The fire on both wings died out in the rush of air.

Nobody said anything for a moment.

Then Obi-Wan cleared his throat.

"And now, for the hard part," he said.

CHAPTER EIGHTEEN

They decided they could not risk flying over the valley. The Sith Lord had been a step ahead of them since they'd arrived on Korriban. He knew they were coming. They would just have to arrive in a way he didn't expect.

They would walk in.

Anakin landed the now-battered speeder on a rocky mountain ledge, squeezing it between the mountain wall and a sheer drop. The Valley of the Dark Lords was a short distance down the mountainside.

They descended the cliffside, hiking quickly but conserving their energy for what lay ahead. The mountains were steep and crowded together like spiteful beasts, with cliffs pressing in from both sides. Occasionally boulders would crash down without warning, sending them leaping for safety. The extended dusk was still holding, but the light was gradually fading. The coming darkness was faintly tinged with red.

When at last they saw the Valley of Dark Lords ahead in the distance, their steps slowed and then stopped. The wave that came at them made them pause. It fractured the Force they felt around them, tore at it. They had expected to feel more of the dark side, but they hadn't realized how concentrated it would be.

They knew the Sith tombs that inhabited the valley were designed to amplify dark energy. It was a physical presence that the Jedi could feel, pressing against their chests. It made them instinctively reach for their lightsaber hilts.

The wind picked up, grabbing at their cloaks with icy fingers. The red-tinged clouds collided, rolling across the sky with a new velocity. They were alone in the middle of a harsh landscape, and even the rocks had warned them to stay away. The sand seemed to suck at their footsteps and the wind was blowing them backward. The air tasted rank and spoiled.

Obi-Wan wanted to say something. There had to be a phrase to bolster them, to make them feel less marooned in this land of gloom and shadows.

It was Ry-Gaul who spoke.

"May the Force be with us."

And, of course, it was this phrase that renewed them, the one they had spoken so many times — to each other, to their Padawans — the words that felt so comfortable in their mouths, the words that were more than words, that lived in their dreams.

They walked on.

They paused just outside the entrance to the valley. The cliffs were so close that they could not all stand in a row. Shelves of razor-sharp rock protruded from each cliff face in a staggered pattern, all the way to the top, so that a craft could not possibly maneuver to get inside. The rock shelves created deep shadows, gray shading into black.

Obi-Wan examined the sides of the entrance carefully. He could see no evidence of weapons or security measures. It seemed impossible to him that they could just walk in.

"There has to be a trap," he said. "Madame Nu says that legend claims that the tombs were guarded by tuk'ata beasts. They were at the service of the Sith."

"Tuk'ata?" Ferus asked.

"Gigantic creatures. Triple rows of teeth, six inch claws, and three horns," Obi-Wan explained. "They can move on four legs or two, and have two winglike extensions — not functional wings, but poisonous stingers. Very fast."

"Let's see," Darra said. "Stingers, claws, teeth, horns. My favorite kind of creature."

"It's a legend, remember?" Anakin said, trying to keep his voice light.

"I . . . don't . . . think so," Tru said, his eyes on the cliffs.

There, the shadows formed into beasts that slowly rose, stretching long necks and sniffing the air.

They were certainly tuk'ata, and they reared up — four, then six, then ten. Their cries seem to split the clouds open. Blood-tinged saliva dripped from their triple rows of teeth. With a flex of their powerful legs, they leaped down from ledge to ledge, and then made the final drop with ease, landing easily and rearing up once again on their hind legs in preparation to attack.

"Did I mention they can jump?" Obi-Wan asked.

The Jedi raised their lightsabers.

CHAPTER NINETEEN

The vicious tuk'ata moved at lightning speed. They did not have an attack strategy. They didn't need one. They charged with flashing teeth and claws and whipping stingers.

Anakin jumped toward the lead tuk'ata. He wanted to be the first to bring one down. The beast whirled, its yellow eyes flat with menace. One massive claw swiped through the air. Anakin caught it with his lightsaber. The beast howled. He had only angered it.

He needed to hit a vulnerable spot. He saw Ferus and Siri attack a tuk'ata together, moving in rhythm. Perhaps he should have waited for his own Master, but with a quick look over his shoulder Anakin saw that Obi-Wan was occupied with two tuk'ata at once, while Ry-Gaul and Tru were racing to help.

The creature swiped at him again, and, anticipating the move, Anakin ducked and rolled, trying to strike up into the beast's chest, where he assumed a blow would kill it. To his surprise, the stinger landed on his arm. He had not expected that range of motion. Instantly, his arm was on fire, though the stinger had barely licked him. Anakin flipped his lightsaber to his other hand, cursing his luck.

The tuk'ata struck, no doubt following up on his advantage. While its prey was immobilized by the poison, the beast would finish him off. But Anakin was able to flip backward and strike, this time burying his lightsaber in the middle of the creature's head. He heard the sizzle and smelled the smoke. The yellow eyes rolled, and the creature fell dead.

Ry-Gaul and Tru had been outflanked by two tuk'ata. Obi-Wan had his hands full with one massive beast, bigger and fiercer than the rest. Anakin leaped on the back of the tuk'ata bearing down on his Master, hoping to distract it. The beast reared up, both stingers waving, while Anakin did a quick and elusive dance to avoid their sting.

Obi-Wan advanced, striking the tuk'ata with a series of hard blows. The creature staggered. Anakin was able to slash at the creature's neck before he was thrown off. The tuk'ata screamed, rearing, and Anakin and Obi-

Wan leaped out of its way. It toppled and thrashed and then was still.

They were already moving, turning to charge one of the tuk'ata who was after Tru. With a roar, it turned on them instead, circling and striking, trying to get claws and teeth embedded into Obi-Wan. Obi-Wan used his liquid cable launcher and anchored it on the creature's horn. Using the cable, he swung up and out, his lightsaber a blur of motion as he attacked again and again. The creature howled, trying to claw Obi-Wan away. Anakin was able to deliver the death blow in the chest.

Obi-Wan swung off the creature and landed, his boots thudding on the dirt. The cries of the tuk'ata mingled with the buzz of lightsabers as the Jedi met their attacks with moves and counter-moves. The tide of the battle was turning. Five tuk'ata lay dead, and two were mortally wounded. Anakin and Obi-Wan were able to team up with Ry-Gaul and Tru first alternately feinting to confuse the creature, and then slicing it into several pieces. Soara and Darra, working together in their usual flawless teamwork, had somehow kept two tuk'ata at bay. Wounded, the two counterattacked, but Darra and Soara were too fast, too agile, and too strong.

At last all the tuk'ata lay dead or dying, their cries echoing off the stones of the mountain.

"So much for legends," Anakin said, sheathing his lightsaber.

Now they were able to simply walk through the narrow passage and enter the valley. But the dark side slammed into them, a body blow. For a moment, they paused to fight the feeling, pulling in the Force to cushion it.

The mausoleums marched down the valley. Hewed from slabs of the mountain, polished by slaves, and then battered by the elements over hundreds of years, they were still enormous, high and wide, with columns and turrets. Mammoth statues, similar to those in the landing hangar, posed like guards outside the tombs. On the cliff summits, ancient statues of horrible creatures perched, appearing ready to strike. It was a valley designed to strike fear into every heart.

"We'll have to search every tomb," Soara said.

"Oh, good," Darra breathed under her breath.

Obi-Wan glanced at Anakin. "You're hurt," he said, concerned.

"It's nothing."

"This is only the beginning of the battle, Anakin," Obi-Wan warned sternly. "Let me treat it."

Anakin bared his arm. Quickly, Obi-Wan administered bacta. The burning sensation lessened somewhat. Anakin felt the coolness of the medicine on his skin. Gratefully, he shrugged his arm back into his tunic. He thanked his Master with his gaze.

He heard something — whispering voices, just as he'd heard upon his arrival. He could see that the others heard them, too. Low, guttural, insistent. Yet what were they saying? It was impossible to tell. Something evil. Something he did not wish to hear.

"They are waking," Ry-Gaul said.

"They know we're here," Siri agreed.

The dead Sith Lords, slumbering inside the huge stone mausoleums, had felt the Jedi presence. The dark energy poured out of the tombs. Anakin could taste it all, anger and cruelty and pain.

"Let's try the first tomb," Obi-Wan said.

He's not there! Anakin wanted to cry. But he didn't know how he knew it. He couldn't trust it. It could be the Sith, trying to confuse him.

Frustration coiled inside him. He hated this feeling. He wanted to be able to trust what he knew. And he wanted to know everything. That would be true power.

"Stay together," Soara said.

The tomb was massive. Two stone creatures guarded it, teeth bared, claws in attack position. Now Anakin recognized them as tuk'ata. Obi-Wan pressed against the stone door, and it groaned as it opened. They walked inside, keeping close together, their lightsabers

108

held in position, serving as illumination as well as defense.

The tombs ran along the wall, slabs of stone with life-sized carved stone figures resting on top representing the dead Sith Lords. The whispers in the air grew louder. Anakin felt them against his skin like little puffs of foul air.

Trespass don't we power Sith darkness command merciless . . .

Anakin heard random words, hissed in hate. He called on the Force to help him turn the words into meaningless static.

The darkness was absolute. The glow of their lightsabers barely penetrated it. They walked another few steps.

Suddenly, Darra cried out. A human skeleton rose out of the dark corner and slammed into her, knocking her to the floor. The bones trapped her like a cage. She tried to slash at them with her lightsaber but couldn't move her arm.

Soara's lightsaber whipped through the air. In seconds, the bones were dust. She stepped forward to help Darra.

"Careful —" Obi-Wan began.

It was too late. An energy net fell from the ceiling, trapping Soara and Darra. At the same time, blasterfire pinged throughout the tomb in a zigzag fashion. They couldn't tell where it was coming from.

Obi-Wan leaped to protect Soara and Darra. Tru and Ry-Gaul moved forward, trying to detect the source of the fire. Anakin followed while Ferus and Siri slashed at the energy net, trying to release them.

From the rear of the tomb, a fireball erupted. It rolled toward them, fast and deadly.

"We have to get out of here!" Obi-Wan shouted.

Soara began to kick free of the net, grabbing Darra's arm and hauling her out. The Jedi hurtled toward the door. It was sealed tight.

They were trapped.

CHAPTER TWENTY

There was nowhere to go but up. The heat of the fireball singed them as they leaped. It hurtled under them and smashed against the door. The Jedi were able to hang in the air, using the Force, for the crucial seconds they needed. They watched in astonishment as the fire blasted through the closed door. Corrosive, annihilating, the fire ate through stone.

The Jedi landed on the still burning ashes and made it outside. The fire burned itself out until it was just a pile of ash on the floor.

"Are you all right?" Soara asked Darra.

Darra nodded, but she still looked shaky from the electrical pulses in the stun net.

Obi-Wan knew one thing. They could not search

every tomb like this. They would lose their energy, lose their focus.

He faced the tombs. He reached out, feeling each dark place, sending his concentration to every corner.

He felt him again. Omega was close now to his goal. Obi-Wan smelled his triumph.

He turned. "There." He pointed down the row. "Zan Arbor and Omega are in there. They've gone to meet the Sith."

Singed by the fire, bloodied by the tuk'ata, they moved as one body toward the tomb Obi-Wan had indicated.

Anakin knew he was there. The Sith was somewhere in the vast tomb. He was waiting. He was watching. But Omega didn't interest him. The Jedi did.

When they entered, it seemed even darker than the first tomb had been. The air was close and smelled of decay. The tombs here were in worse shape, crumbling, some of them decayed so much that they could see the bodies inside wrapped in shrouds.

Obi-Wan held up his lightsaber. From its glow they could see pictographs on the walls, images scrawled in red that had faded. Images of deeds done by the Sith. Wars. Massacres. Anakin turned his face away.

Join us darkness conquer dominance glory . . .

Anakin saw one of the shrouds rise. The layers of gray, shredding rags fell away. He gasped in shock. It was his mother, Shmi.

"*Annie*," she called. "*Annie*."

"Mother." The word was wrenched out of his belly. How much had he longed to say that word again, to see her again? It was the Jedi who kept him from her, the Jedi who had taken him away. . . .

"Anakin!" Obi-Wan's voice was sharp. "It's a vision. Nothing more."

Anakin swallowed. The shroud was back in the crypt. He gazed at the others, embarrassed. Ferus looked at him with pity. Pity! His hatred for Ferus flooded him again. He had embarrassed himself in front of Ferus!

The visions came to all of them then. Sith Lords rose and walked toward them, their mouths gaping, their hands grasping, and then disintegrated onto them with foul smells and tastes. The Jedi walked on, through the corpse visions, through the whispers, through the taunts.

You are blind and you are fools and you understand nothing. . . .

The dark side of the Force was like a thick curtain Anakin couldn't draw aside. It got in his mouth and eyes and felt as though it could slow his hands, stop his legs. Still, he kept on walking, kept on moving. There was nothing else to be done. They had to get to the end of it.

The creatures carved from stone that sat on the ledges took flight in shimmering images of fire and destruction. Tru ducked as one of them flew directly in his face, but the creature became nothing but particles of dust. Anakin saw Tru grip his lightsaber more tightly.

Tru's lightsaber! He had forgotten to tell him to check the readout for the flux aperture! He had walked away, angry and hurt. Why hadn't he remembered?

Had he *wanted* to forget?

He couldn't do it now. If he did, the Masters would know that Tru's lightsaber had broken and he hadn't told Ry-Gaul. He would get himself and Tru in trouble. And Ferus probably had fixed it perfectly, the way he did everything else.

What you are and what you do mean nothing next to what we are and can do. . . .

Thinking of Ferus made anger spurt through Anakin. It was something hard inside him. It filled him up. It felt natural, it felt right, to allow his anger to grow. Why had he tried to quell it? He had every right to feel it! Just feeling it now gave him strength.

Obi-Wan held up a hand. "Stop. Energy trap."

Anakin could see nothing. Everything was dark except for the light from Obi-Wan's lightsaber.

Obi-Wan spoke in a hushed tone. "Concentrations of dark power. They are capable of immobilizing a Jedi for a time."

"I don't see anything," Ferus said.

"Look away, then look back. Use the Force," Siri instructed.

Anakin looked away, then looked back. He caught the faintest shimmer of purple in the air. It appeared and disappeared. You could miss it if you blinked.

"I see it," Darra said.

"There will be more," Obi-Wan warned. "The Padawans must be very careful. You most likely won't be able to escape alone. Stay close to your Masters."

They moved forward, avoiding the trap.

The chuckle split the fetid air.

"I would expect no less of you, Obi-Wan." The voice came out of nowhere. Mocking, sure of himself.

Granta Omega.

Obi-Wan stopped.

Slowly, Omega walked out from behind a tomb, just meters ahead.

He tapped a finger on his utility belt. "Did you really think you could avoid a few traps and catch me?"

"Get back here, you fool," Zan Arbor hissed, appearing behind him out of the darkness. "Why must you always *talk* to him?" In her blue shimmersilk, she looked as well-kept as ever, her blond hair piled in a profusion of neat braids on her head.

"Because I'm enjoying myself," Omega said. His handsome face creased in a wide smile. He appeared utterly at home in the terrible tomb. "I have, let's see — one, two, four, *eight* Jedi, all sent to capture little old me!"

"Are you forgetting I'm here, too?" Zan Arbor snapped. "Typical. I was a Jedi enemy before you were born, Granta."

"My father was their enemy before me," Omega said.

Xanatos. Omega's father, the former Jedi who had tried to destroy Qui-Gon. Obi-Wan had told Anakin about him. His son maintained the same arrogance, the same cruelty, the same howling need to hurt the Jedi, to make them pay for everything they lacked themselves. Honor meant nothing to either Xanatos or Omega. Only power. Only revenge.

Zan Arbor waved a hand. "This isn't a contest. I'm going on. Sith or no Sith, I can't wait to get off this planet. Come along. He's waiting for us. Come *on*," she urged sharply. "He'll take care of the Jedi — he promised us that. He's about to give us everything we worked for. Resources. Secrets of the galaxy. Wealth. An army of our own, Granta!"

But Omega didn't move. Here would come his downfall, Anakin thought suddenly. The reward he was about to receive meant nothing in the face of his personal revenge.

"I can take care of this," Omega said. "With his help."

"Can I remind you of something?" Zan Arbor exploded in exasperation. *"You are not a Sith!"*

"I have surprised you every step of the way, Obi-Wan," Omega said, ignoring her. "And I didn't even know the secrets of the dark side! Can you imagine what I'm capable of now, in this place, where the very walls are your enemy?"

Obi-Wan held his gaze. Anakin glanced at him. He saw that Obi-Wan had no desire to speak. In his gaze Anakin detected no anger, no response to Omega's taunts. There was simply the grim will to get this done. There was no way Omega was leaving this tomb unless Obi-Wan led him out.

"Don't want to talk to me, Obi-Wan? Giving me the silent treatment? You're spoiling my pleasure." Omega gave a theatrical sigh and raised his hand, revealing a KYD-21 blaster. Anakin recognized it. Fast, precise, compact.

"I must admit, it's inconvenient that the Jedi found me here. But in a way, it's such a delicious end. I'm invincible now, you see. I fight with the power of the Sith behind me. And that means I can watch you die, Obi-Wan. You and your apprentice. I can't wait. Do you want to follow me back there, or are you too afraid to finally meet your defeat?"

He had gotten no further than a flex of one finger muscle to fire before Obi-Wan exploded in movement. He raced toward Omega, his lightsaber held in a classic offensive maneuver.

The blaster bolts came fast and furious. Obi-Wan deflected each one, swinging his lightsaber in a wide arc.

A horrid stench suddenly rolled out from behind Omega. He smiled, as if he knew what was coming. No doubt he did.

Then the undead came. Korriban zombies, revived by the Sith to guard the tombs. Anakin had read about them, but never thought he'd see them; the Sith must have activated them to defend Omega and the sacred Sith ground. The zombies were used to eating the flesh from the tombs; now they had living targets in mind. And they had blasters and detonators to make the kill. They came careening out of the darkness now, different species but all moving with the same odd, lurching gait . . . the air came alive with smoke and fire.

Recovering from a moment of shock, Anakin moved to flank Obi-Wan. The zombies had strength beyond the living. They were half-rotted, a horrifying sight. Anakin did not look at their dead gazes. He went after them ruthlessly, his lightsaber deflecting their fire while he cut them to ribbons.

They were an obstacle, nothing more. A sorcerer's trick from long ago. He would not let their gruesome appearance or their grasping bloodied hands deter him.

He had to be in on the capture of Omega. Working together, he and Obi-Wan deflected fire while they moved toward a steadily retreating Omega. Zan Arbor had disappeared. For Anakin, she had ceased to matter.

Then the darkness came alive with visions. The Sith Lords, mighty in their armor, terrifying in their decaying, bloodied faces. They rushed at the Jedi, only to disappear in a shower of splintered shadow. Anakin tried not to flinch, to keep his eyes on the blaster fire, but the confusion was everywhere.

The dark side of the Force was like a presence, interfering with concentration and sapping energy. The Jedi reached out to one another, calling on the Force to battle the dark side, the undead who kept on coming.

Anakin saw Shmi rise and fall, rise and fall. He felt the familiar need, the familiar guilt. The feelings overwhelmed him and Obi-Wan had to leap in front of him to protect him from a detonator heading his way. Obi-Wan swiped it out of the air.

They didn't choose me, and yet I fight for them, Anakin thought in anger. *They chose Ferus, and yet I must fight to protect him, protect them. My Master didn't protect me, why am I doing this?*

A phantom Sith Lord smiled at him. Reached out a hand.

"Anakin." Obi-Wan's voice was close. "Keep your focus."

His focus. Yes. Of course the dark side would go after him, not just with phantom Sith, but phantoms in his brain. Thoughts that weren't his. Anakin reached out to the Force to help him battle the voices. He felt his head clear.

Tru had leaped up on a tomb to fight two zombies. With his flexible arms and legs, he moved like a rolling wave. He took down three thermal detonators that were flying through the air. He swung his lightsaber in an arc. It flickered. Anakin watched in horror as it buzzed, the shaft flickering again and again. It was losing power!

Tru was in the middle of them. Obi-Wan hadn't seen it. He had charged forward, the way to Omega now clear.

Everything in Anakin screamed to follow Obi-Wan, to be in on the capture of Omega. Except one thing.

Friendship.

But he had hesitated too long. As he watched, Ferus and Tru exchanged a glance. Simultaneously, Ferus and Tru flipped their lightsabers through the air. Tru caught Ferus's, and Ferus caught Tru's.

Re-energized, Tru went after the undead, hacking off limbs and disabling the living corpses. Ferus dropped to a backup position with the half-powered lightsaber.

But suddenly Omega appeared again. He had sneaked around the back of the tombs. Zan Arbor reappeared at his side. Anakin realized that they were trying to trick the Jedi. They had set up most of the firepower in the middle of the tomb. While the Jedi expected them to retreat to the rear, they were actually about to escape through the front door.

He saw it again, the flicker at the end of his vision, a cape furling as fast as a serpent's strike. The Sith stood at the entrance to the tomb. Waiting. His face was hidden in the shadow of his hood.

Zan Arbor hurried toward him.

Anakin wrenched his attention back to Tru. Because Ferus was watching Tru's back, he was the only one in Omega's path. The Jedi Masters had all been at the fore of the fight. Ferus's lightsaber flickered in the dark.

Seeing that he was in trouble, Darra Force-leaped toward Ferus, her lightsaber held high, determined to save him.

Anakin saw the smile on Omega's face when he fired.

The bolts hit Darra straight in the chest. She fell, still keeping her body between Omega and Ferus.

Soara cried out. Anakin felt the moment spin out into impossible time, time that froze everything, even his heart.

He saw the blue shimmersilk move like a breeze as Zan Arbor took advantage of the distraction to dash for the entrance. Blue Force-lightning erupted in the darkness, a barrier shielding her from the others, giving her space to run.

He saw Tru's mouth open in a howl. He saw Ferus drop to his knees and crawl toward Darra, saw him take a blaster bolt in the shoulder and keep on going. He saw Siri leap forward to defend all of them, saw Soara fly through the air in a great Force-leap to be near her Padawan. Saw Darra's head turn toward him, her cheek against the dirt. Saw the cloudy film in Darra's eyes, the shock of catching the blow. He saw, as if it were a physical struggle, her gathering her courage to accept the blow.

He saw all this, and still he didn't move.

And then Omega moved, reversing course once again, quickly retreating away from the tomb.

Anguish on his face, Obi-Wan turned away from the Jedi and followed him.

Real time came rushing back, and there was not enough of it.

Anakin turned away from Darra and raced after his Master.

CHAPTER TWENTY-ONE

The tomb narrowed at the rear. The stench almost made Anakin gag. It was as though everything foul was concentrated back here. He could barely make out Obi-Wan ahead, running, attacking the undead that guarded Omega, circling him constantly like a cloud of rotting flesh.

Anakin put on a burst of speed. His Master was battling with incredible speed and accuracy. Anakin could feel the Force like a great pulsing, speeding, enveloping wave that barreled Obi-Wan toward his opponent. Toward his destiny.

My destiny, Anakin thought. *Mine!*

He focused so much on his Master, on his need to catch him, that he blundered into an energy trap.

Anakin was caught. He couldn't move. Frustrated, enraged, he slashed at the invisible cage with his lightsaber. He could not free himself. He kicked. He hammered. Caught.

He had met a power greater than his. Impossible!

"Master!" he called, but Obi-Wan didn't hear him. The energy trap sucked his voice out of the air and imprisoned it.

I just need the Force. Obi-Wan said a Master can summon the Force and fight this. I am as good as a Master. I can do this.

Strange, though. He could reach out for the Force, but visions got in the way. And not visions from the dark side. Visions of what had just happened. Tru's mouth, open in a howl of anguish and disbelief. Darra, falling, eyes wide with the shock.

Darra, her head turned toward him, her cheek in the dust of the tomb.

He had seen her like this before, when she'd been wounded on Haariden. He had felt her wounding then was his fault. Unsure of her abilities, sure of his own, he had leaped to protect her and crashed into her instead. He had thought himself the better fighter, and because of that, he had pushed her into blaster fire.

She had never held it against him.

He saw her face again, so pale. The bright ribbon she always wove through her braid, trailing in the dust of the tomb.

He knew she was badly wounded. He felt it choke him. He had not gone to help Ferus. Darra had. She was lying on the ground. He tried to put those facts together to have them make sense.

Tru's lightsaber had slipped to half-power.

Anakin had never offered to check the flux aperture, just in case. He had meant to.

What is happening to me? Anakin wondered. His mind felt suddenly clear, sharp. *Why didn't I help my friends? Have I changed? Am I changing? What am I becoming?*

When he had first become a Padawan, he would not have hesitated. His first loyalty had been to them.

Things were more complicated now. There was more at stake.

Maybe he was changing for the better.

Control rule supremacy greatness . . .

Was he more mature now? A better fighter? Better able to assess a situation, move toward the goal? Was that why he had raced to confront Omega? Or had his own jealousy propelled him? How could he separate those things? Why did he have to?

Power rules by results . . .

Anakin shook his head. The voices would not leave him.

He thought of Darra. Tenderness filled him, and the voices went away.

Years ago, he had gone to see Darra in the med clinic, filled with remorse. She had shaken him out of his guilt with a grin. *Now I have something to impress the younglings with. I've been wounded in battle.*

And then he remembered something he hadn't thought of in years. He had always thought of her strength during that time. Now he remembered her fragility. He remembered her hand on the coverlet. Her fingers had so briefly touched his sleeve.

Stay with me until I fall asleep. It's lonely here.

Anakin beat at the trap again. He felt the rage rise inside him. He knew the rage was interfering with the Force, but he couldn't control it. If only . . . if only he could *use* the rage. But that was something a Jedi should not do.

The frustration boiled in him. He could not move. His Master was gone now, into the darkness.

Obi-Wan shouldn't have been surprised when the visions of the Sith Lords faded and he saw Qui-Gon. But he was. He should have known the Sith were capable of drawing his most painful memory from within him.

Qui-Gon, with a gaping wound in his chest where Darth Maul had struck.

"You were always so afraid of disappointing me," Qui-Gon said. "And you have."

Obi-Wan stopped. His lightsaber dangled in his hand.

It's not real. It's not real.

"You've failed me, Obi-Wan."

Not . . . real.

"And you don't even know why."

Obi-Wan took a breath. He walked forward, straight at Qui-Gon. The image disappeared.

Shaken, he continued into the darkness. Now it was easier to walk past the Sith Lords, the visions who snarled and hissed and sent out grasping fingers as he walked past. He had seen the worst.

He heard a hiss, felt the dark side surge, and barely had time to prepare when the flash lit up the darkness. A luma blast, sent by a rocket, designed to blind him.

Obi-Wan threw himself on the floor and rolled. Behind his closed eyes, he saw explosions of orange and yellow, bright as a double sun. Using the Force, he guided himself alongside a tomb and crouched behind it. When he opened his eyes, he could see nothing.

Then more blaster fire, so rapid he realized that Omega must have set up a repeating blaster. From the sound of it, an E-Web, one of the most powerful repeating blasters ever manufactured. It sat on a tripod. It took two gunners, but one could handle it, if very skilled.

Omega didn't know where he was . . . yet. Obi-Wan was painfully aware that the E-Web had enough power to punch through armor plating on a cruiser. He heard the stone tombs shatter across the space as they were hit. He couldn't remain here. He had to keep moving.

He kept himself low to the ground and felt his way around the tomb. He could track the blaster fire through the Force, could defend himself if he had to. It was part of Jedi training to be able to fight without sight. Younglings learned with novice helmets that blocked their vision. Obi-Wan was suddenly, fiercely glad for that training.

Omega would expect him to hide. Therefore, he had to expose himself. He had to trust in the Force.

Blinded, Obi-Wan rushed forward. He felt the air against him as a guide. Objects displaced air, and with the help of the Force, a Jedi could feel the displacement and adjust. Obi-Wan raced forward confidently. His vision would return. In the meantime, Omega was close. So close he could hear the creak of his armorweave tunic as he moved his arm. . . .

A wrist rocket. Obi-Wan dodged and weaved, knowing the targeting laser system was working to get a fix on him. He moved like quicksilver, flowing from one position to the next. He heard the rocket release and he put on a burst of speed, running blind, running straight at Omega now. He felt the whistle as the rocket whizzed by his ear.

"I love watching you run," Omega said. "Ready, set, go!"

Another wrist rocket. Obi-Wan Force-leaped. He felt the rocket behind him and he swerved at the last minute. The rocket crashed into a tomb. Splinters of rock showered over Obi-Wan.

"I could do this all day," Omega said.

Blinded, breathing hard, Obi-Wan allowed himself a fraction of a moment to rest. Inside him blazed the memory of every battle with Omega. From the beginning Omega had set out to confound him, humiliate him, destroy him. He had set out to impress the Sith by attacking the Jedi, and he had managed to do it again and again, always escaping at the last possible moment. He had even managed to kill a Jedi Master. Yaddle had sacrificed her life for this man's greed and revenge.

It had to end here. It had to end now.

He saw streaks in his vision now, a sign that his sight was returning. He just needed a few precious minutes.

"You mentioned having the help of the Sith, Omega," Obi-Wan said, raising his voice to carry without shouting. "How is that you've ended up alone back here?"

"I'm not alone," Omega said. "I have his help."

"Really? Can you feel him? I can't. And remember, I'm the one who can feel the Force. Not you."

"You arrogant fool," Omega snarled. "I am to be a Sith! He told me so."

"And you believed him." Obi-Wan was beginning to make out the shape of the tomb opposite him, fragments of shape fracturing the orange streaks in his vision. "Flattery will get him everywhere, it seems."

"He wasn't flattering me! Right now I am a Sith without the Force. I can use *his* power." There was a note of defensiveness in Omega's voice.

"It seems to me that he gets to use you."

"He would not abandon me!"

The shapes took sharper form. His vision wasn't perfect, but it would have to do.

Obi-Wan stood. "You'd better hope so."

He could just barely make out Omega standing behind the E-Web. "Your arrogance will bring you down, Obi-Wan!"

"Funny. I was just about to say the same." Obi-Wan activated his lightsaber again. The blaster bolts were so powerful they sent shock waves down his arm as he deflected them. The fire was fast and furious. Where was Anakin? He could use his help. Or someone's . . .

He had to concentrate on the moment. Not on what he didn't have.

You have everything you need, my Padawan.

This time, Qui-Gon's voice was kind. The voice was inside him. It was true, it was real, and it gave him strength.

His lightsaber whirled, spinning in an arc to gather momentum with each strike against the bolts. He could hear Omega breathing heavily. Obi-Wan was sending bolts back to him at a steady pace, but Omega was managing to evade fire as he deployed the E-Web repeating blaster.

The orange streaks were fading now. Obi-Wan could clearly see the outlines of the last tombs. Omega was silhouetted against the blaster bolts that sent faint, electric illumination through the air. He was gripping the blaster on the tripod, intent now in the full fury of his lust to take Obi-Wan down.

Something Anakin had once said floated through his mind. Anakin knew more about machines than Obi-Wan ever wanted to know.

Funny. No matter how advanced, a weapon always has a flaw. It can always turn against itself.

The flaw. What was the flaw?

The E-Web needed two operators because it was liable to overload if one operator didn't keep track of power flow. If overloaded, it wouldn't simply shut down — it would backblast.

Obi-Wan put on another burst of speed. He went after each blaster bolt with skilled parries. But instead of advancing he moved laterally. He only appeared to advance.

Out of rockets now, Omega tore off the wrist launchers. They were heavy, and he was getting tired. Sweat was pouring down his face. The E-Web was smoking now, and he didn't notice.

Obi-Wan's arms began to shake from the effort of deflecting the blaster bolts. He was tired. His vision was still faulty. With sudden clarity, he realized that he could lose this battle. He was calculating on the failure of a machine he wasn't terribly familiar with. He was counting on a bit of luck.

It took all of his concentration. One stumble could send him straight into a blaster bolt that would rip through him like pudding.

Through the smoke, across the haze, Omega's blue gaze was hot and burning. Hate blazed at Obi-Wan. Omega was screaming incoherently now, his voice barely heard over the sound of gunfire. The E-Web pounded and smoked.

Obi-Wan stumbled and hit his knees. Omega smiled. He leaned forward to aim.

The weapon gave in. It shuddered and stopped for one small instant. Omega shook it.

The blast was tremendous. A concentration of energy blew Omega back, his body dangling in the air, a shocked expression on his face. He slammed into the tomb wall. Broken. The shock on his face faded as his life drained from him.

"You . . ." It was all he managed to get out.

Obi-Wan heard pounding feet behind him. Anakin ran up and stopped. "Master —"

"It's all right. He's gone." Obi-Wan deactivated his lightsaber. "It's over."

"I was caught in an energy trap."

"You got out by yourself. That's good. Come, Padawan." Obi-Wan turned. "Let's see to the others. We —"

A gathering roar came from behind him. Omega threw himself forward, a blaster firing in his hand, his teeth bared. "You killed my father! You . . . will . . . not . . . win!"

Obi-Wan activated his lightsaber as he turned. The moment he had not wanted to come had arrived. No matter how much he had wished to stop Omega, he had never wished to kill him. He remembered how Xanatos's death had haunted Qui-Gon. He did not want the same fate.

But fate had taken away his choices.

His lightsaber rose, as if in slow motion. Yet it moved faster than an eyeblink. It came down and cleaved into Omega.

He fell to his knees.

Instead of retreating, Obi-Wan walked forward. He did not want to see Omega die, but no one should have to die alone.

Omega looked up into his face. His lips were drawn back over his teeth in a gruesome smile. A spasm of something crossed his features. What was it? Satisfaction, Obi-Wan realized. What did it mean?

"Do you think you won? You didn't," Omega said. Every word was an effort. "I know . . . who he is." He toppled over, curling up like a child. "You will wish . . . you did."

Still smiling, still holding his hatred and rage, Omega let go of his life at last and collapsed into the dust.

Something rushed out, as if a great power had removed its protection from Omega.

The visions of the Sith Lords faded. The dark side of

the Force retreated. The Sith would not be found. Obi-Wan knew he had withdrawn both his presence and his protection.

Obi-Wan tucked his lightsaber back into his belt. "Let's see to Darra," he said.

Soara cradled her in her arms. Tru had wrapped his cloak around her. Ferus sat on the ground, his head in his hands, and did not look up. Siri and Ry-Gaul stood on either side of the group, as if guarding them from harm. But harm had come and done its work.

Darra was dead.

Obi-Wan knelt in front of her. Her eyes were closed, her face composed and impossibly calm. Anakin watched as Soara very gently unraveled Darra's Padawan braid. She plucked the bright ribbon from the coils of soft hair and held it in her fist. Tears streaked down her face. Anakin could never have imagined seeing Soara Antana, fabled warrior, in tears.

Anakin heard Darra's voice rise like a cry inside him. *Stay with me until I fall asleep. It's lonely here.*

CHAPTER TWENTY-TWO

The Great Hall seemed more vast, the journey to the Council room longer than Obi-Wan ever remembered. His legs had never felt so heavy. He walked without seeing. He felt strangely numb. He had never felt so tired.

He knew about the rumors at the Temple. He knew that Tru's lightsaber had been faulty, that Ferus had fixed it secretly, that neither of them had told their Masters. He knew that Tru had been censured. Ferus was in seclusion but would be facing the Council directly after Obi-Wan.

He knew these things, and he knew that in the eyes of the Council, the mission had succeeded, in part. They had caught Granta Omega. Zan Arbor had escaped, but the Council felt she was easier to track.

Without Omega's wealth, she would not find it easy to hide.

They had missed uncovering the identity of the Sith, but the Council did not fault them. They had been close to him. They had uncovered one of the planets that sheltered him. They had taken a small step forward.

He should feel some sense of satisfaction, but he did not. Obi-Wan found himself wondering about things he had not thought about since Qui-Gon's death.

Was the loss of Darra's life worth what they had obtained?

Was there something he should have done that he did not do?

Had the first vision of Qui-Gon in the tomb come from the Sith, or deep within him?

Had he failed?

Darra's death would once have been an aberration. Why did he feel it was a portent? With every second that passed, he felt more death approach. Time and again he had to shake off the memory of Granta Omega curling up like a child as he let go of life. What could he have been, if he had not been in the grip of his obsession? The Sith found weakness and exploited it. They took a flaw and twisted it into a weapon. Whoever the Sith was, he had goaded Omega, used him, and abandoned him. How could the

Jedi fight someone who had no mercy for anyone or anything?

Over the last few days, Anakin had retreated to the Map Room where he liked to meditate. Obi-Wan couldn't put his finger on it, but he felt that somehow Anakin was involved in what had happened to Darra. Not directly, but somehow . . .

He hated himself for having this feeling. Of course, if that were true his Padawan would have told him.

Obi-Wan found himself outside the Council Room doors. He tried to clear his mind before he entered. Some days it was difficult meeting so many Jedi gifted in Force-sensitivity at once.

The doors slid open. The full Council had assembled. The members all acknowledged Obi-Wan as he took his place in the middle of the room, where he had stood so many times.

"A sad conclusion to the mission, it was," Yoda said. "Grieving are all of us."

"Darra Thel-Tanis has joined the Force," Mace said. "We will celebrate her life."

"Uneasy we are with the conduct of the two Padawans, Ferus Olin and Tru Veld," Yoda said.

Adi Gallia nodded. "We have reconsidered our decision to speed up the trials for chosen Padawans. We fear we put too much pressure on them."

"We need additional Jedi, it's true," Oppo Rancisis said. "But we see now that we cannot rush readiness."

"Our mistake, it was," Yoda said.

"Mistakes we cannot afford during these times," Mace added, and then said, "We will commend your Padawan for his bravery. To face a Sith is the hardest task for a Jedi. Anakin showed ingenuity and bravery throughout the mission."

Yoda peered at Obi-Wan. "Something to share with us, you have?"

Obi-Wan hesitated. He had doubts. He had fears. He had sorrows. But this was not the place.

"No, Master Yoda," he said.

"Disappointed your Padawan will be, to hear that we have cancelled our plans to accelerate Knighthood," Yoda said.

"Yes, Anakin will be disappointed," Obi-Wan said. "He is not good at waiting."

"Then wait, he should," Yoda said, nodding.

"Thank you, Master Kenobi," Mace said. "You may send in Ferus Olin."

Obi-Wan bowed and retreated. When he walked into the outer chamber, Ferus stood.

"They are ready for you," Obi-Wan told him.

Ferus turned a face to him full of such misery and heartbreak that Obi-Wan was moved.

"You are not here to be punished, least of all by yourself," Obi-Wan told him.

"I must go on living," Ferus responded. "That is my punishment."

CHAPTER TWENTY-THREE

Anakin waited until he saw Obi-Wan leave the outer chamber. He wasn't ready to talk to his Master yet. He waited until Obi-Wan was gone, then slipped inside.

He didn't want to see Ferus face-to-face, but he had to find out what was going on. What would the Council do? Now, of all times, Anakin felt a strange attachment to his fellow Padawan.

The shock of Darra's death hadn't worn off. He still couldn't grasp it. He still couldn't believe it wasn't possible to see her again, to hear her voice. If the Force was so powerful, why couldn't it stop death? Why couldn't he break through that wall and see his friend again?

He felt a rustle behind him, and saw Tru backing out of the chamber.

"Tru!" Anakin called. Reluctantly, Tru edged in a few steps. "Do you know anything?"

Tru shook his head. He didn't quite meet Anakin's eyes.

"I haven't seen much of you since we've been back," Anakin said.

"I know."

"I'm sorry about the censure."

"I deserved it."

The question burned on Anakin's tongue. "Why did you go to Ferus instead of me to fix your lightsaber? I would have done a better job."

"I didn't go to Ferus," Tru said. "He came to me. He had noticed that it was on half-power at the end of the battle in the monastery. But I wouldn't have gone to you because I wouldn't have wanted to get you in trouble. You would have kept my secret. Just like Ferus did. I was wrong not to tell my Master. I was wrong to let Ferus stay silent. I was just about as wrong as I could be."

"You were thinking of the mission," Anakin said.

"We were all wrong," Tru continued, as if he hadn't even registered what Anakin had said.

"We did our best," Anakin said. "And Omega is dead."

"So is Darra."

Tru turned and walked out.

Anakin started after him. Something was wrong. Something had changed between him and his friend, and he didn't know why.

He stopped when the Council doors opened. Ferus walked out. He almost walked by Anakin without seeing him, as though he was blinded by his feelings.

"Ferus?"

Ferus turned. "Anakin. Well. I think you should be the first to know. I have resigned from the Jedi Order."

"What?!" Anakin felt shock ripple through him. "But why?"

"Because I was responsible for Darra's death."

"That's not true! You couldn't have known —"

"But I did. I knew that Tru's lightsaber had malfunctioned. I offered to fix it secretly. I did not tell his Master or urge him to do so. His lightsaber failed in battle, and Darra was killed trying to protect me."

"But you thought you'd fixed it!"

Ferus stopped. He gazed at Anakin for a long moment.

"You knew?" he asked. "You knew Tru's lightsaber had broken? You must have seen me fixing it."

"I didn't say that."

"No. You didn't. But there are only the two of us here, Anakin. You don't have to lie."

Anakin said nothing. As usual, Ferus was trying to trap him, trying to show Anakin how much nobler he was.

"When we got back, I took it to the Jedi Master Tolan Hing," Ferus said, naming the Jedi who was known for his expertise in the workings of a lightsaber. "He told me that that the fusing between the flux aperture and the power cell needed a slight adjustment. Nothing major — Tru might never have noticed it. Except that in battle, the power drained faster than normal."

"I don't know why you're telling me this. . . ."

Tru's voice came from behind him. "Because you fixed the flux aperture. And you would have known that it needed to be rechecked after the power cell boost."

Anakin turned. "You didn't come to me!"

Tru shook his head. "That's funny. Shouldn't you have said, *But I didn't know it was broken?*"

"You're trying to trap me," Anakin said. "Both of you," he added, with an angry look at Ferus. "Tru, I would never do anything deliberately to put you in a position . . ."

Tru's face hardened. His silver eyes held a sheen Anakin had never seen before. They were icy, as though Anakin could slip off his gaze.

"I wondered," Tru said. "When we got back here, I wondered if you knew. I saw how you froze in the tomb.

'But not my friend,' I said to myself. 'My friend would not do that.' But then I thought about how you feel about Ferus, how angry you had been. You would want him to get in trouble, even if it meant exposing me."

"That's not fair!"

"And suddenly I realized — *yes, Anakin could have done that.*"

"You're looking at this all wrong," Anakin said. But how could he explain? He couldn't admit that he knew that Tru's lightsaber was broken because he couldn't explain why he'd forgotten to tell him to readjust it. He still didn't know how he'd forgotten something so crucial. Tru would think he'd deliberately forgotten it.

There was nothing he could say to convince him otherwise, because he himself didn't know.

"I don't think so," Tru said. "I think I'm truly seeing you for the first time."

Anakin swallowed. He didn't know what to say. This was an unfamiliar Tru, not the friend of his childhood.

"I'll see you outside," Tru said to Ferus, and walked out.

"Do you see what you've done?" Anakin said, turning savagely to Ferus.

"Yes, I see what I've done," Ferus said. "Do you?"

He shook his head. "I'm afraid for you. You think admitting you were wrong opens you up to attack."

"That's not true," Anakin countered. "I think you should save your fears for yourself."

A spasm of pain crossed Ferus's face. Anakin could not imagine how awful it must feel, to give up the Jedi Order. It would be like giving up everything he lived for.

"If the Jedi ever need me, I will be there," Ferus said quietly. "That includes you, Anakin."

Ferus walked away quickly. Anakin looked after him angrily. Ferus got the last word. Not only that, but it had been a kind one. The noble Padawan to the last.

Not a Padawan, though. Not any longer.

Satisfaction soon curdled into frustration. Anakin felt as though he'd been beaten, but he didn't know why. He remembered the helplessness he'd felt in the energy trap. He never wanted to feel that way again. Yet he was trapped in his envy, in his anger, just as surely. Even if Ferus left the Temple forever, he would still remember this feeling.

No. The feeling would fade. He would make it fade. He would push it down, down with his memories of Shmi. Now that Ferus was gone, Anakin could fulfill his promise. He would bring balance to the Force.

Tru was angry at him, but he had never truly understood the burden that Anakin carried. Maybe Tru had never understood him at all. Maybe no one did, except for his Master. Tru would come around.

Anakin walked out. At the far end of the hallway, he saw Ferus join Tru.

He felt as though he was watching them through the wrong end of electrobinoculars. They seemed so small, so far away.

Feeling his presence, Tru looked back over his shoulder at Anakin. And then it hit him like a punch that knocked the air from his lungs. Tru would never come around. He'd lost his friend forever.

Standing still, he watched Ferus and Tru walk away.

He heard footsteps beside him, and Obi-Wan was next to him.

"Anakin, I've been looking for you."

He turned automatically. "Do you need me?"

"No, I . . . Anakin? Is something wrong?"

"Ferus has resigned from the Jedi Order."

Obi-Wan let out a breath. "I was afraid he would do something . . . like that. He feels Darra's death so strongly." There was a lost look in Obi-Wan's eyes as he gazed down the empty hallway. "The legacy of this mission is pain."

Anakin wanted to take away the remote look on his

Master's face. He didn't want Obi-Wan to care so much about what happened to Ferus. "The legacy of this mission is that a great enemy has been defeated. I saw you strike him down."

"That is not an act that should bring you satisfaction, my young Padawan," Obi-Wan said sternly. "I took a life."

"It was done as a last resort. And it rid the galaxy of a great evil. Therefore it was necessary and right."

"Necessary — yes. But right?" Obi-Wan shook his head. "That is not a word to throw around lightly. We cannot say what is right. We can only do our best." Obi-Wan's gaze warmed. "As you do, Padawan. You never give less than your best. I'm proud of the Jedi you have become."

Anakin was moved. His Master so rarely spoke this way. "Thank you, Master."

Obi-Wan gave him a long look. "And . . . I wanted to tell you. The Jedi Council has decided that they won't speed up the trials for Padawans. Your Knighthood will have to wait a bit longer."

Anakin absorbed this news. So there was no chance, then. He would have to wait. It didn't matter what he did, how well he performed.

"When the time is right, you'll take the trials, and I

have no doubt that you will astonish us all. Until then, we will work together. There is so much left to do, and I'm grateful to have you by my side for a little longer." Obi-Wan paused. "Anakin? Are you all right?"

He *was* all right, Anakin suddenly realized. The weakness in his knees he'd felt when he saw Tru walk away was gone. In a strange way, the mission had strengthened him. He had a stronger conviction now, a harder edge to fight with. Everything had fallen away from him — his childhood, his friends, his wish to impress the Jedi Council.

He would never be helpless again.

He would only grow stronger.

He had fought with a Sith and seen true power. One day he would be able to match it. He would be able to fight it. Not yet. But someday. Soon.

As a boy, he hadn't wanted things to change. He wanted to keep those he loved close to him forever. Yet everything did change. He was far from his mother. He had lost Darra. Tru. And Qui-Gon. He couldn't fight against those kinds of losses. So be it. He would have to push them down until they didn't matter anymore.

One day, he would face his worst loss, the loss of his Master. By surpassing him, he would lose him. He pictured Obi-Wan turning to him in slow surprise, grasping for the first time the true extent of his power. Seeing that the student had outstripped the teacher.

On that day, Anakin's heart would break for the last time. He would feel the weight of impossible sorrow.

He would not be able to bear that sorrow. Unless he no longer had a heart.